THE MYSTERY OF
HORSESHOE CANYON

THE MYSTERY OF
HORSESHOE CANYON

BY ANN SHELDON

WANDERER BOOKS
Published by Simon & Schuster, New York

Copyright © 1963 by Stratemeyer Syndicate
First Wanderer edition, 1981
Published by WANDERER BOOKS
A Simon & Schuster Division of
Gulf & Western Corporation
Simon & Schuster Building
1230 Avenue of the Americas
New York, New York 10020

Designed by Becky Tachna
Manufactured in the United States of America
10 9 8 7 6 5 4 3 2 1

WANDERER and colophon are trademarks
of Simon & Schuster

LINDA CRAIG is a trademark of Stratemeyer Syndicate

Library of Congress Cataloging in Publication Data

Sheldon, Ann.
Linda Craig, the mystery of Horseshoe Canyon.

Published in 1963 under title: Linda Craig and the
mystery of Horseshoe Canyon.
SUMMARY: Linda, her brother, and two friends
set up a party to search for gem thieves and a legendary
turquoise deposit.
[1. Mystery and detective stories. 2. Ranch life—Fiction]
I. Title. II. Title: The mystery of Horseshoe Canyon.
PZ7.S5413Lj 1981   [Fic]   80-29352

ISBN 0-671-42653-2
ISBN 0-671-42654-0 (pbk.)

Contents

Wild Donkey Hunt   *1*

"How would you two adventurers like to go on a wild donkey hunt?"

At the question, Linda and Bob Craig spun around from the corral fence on which they had been leaning and faced their smiling grandfather.

Linda's dark eyes sparkled with enthusiasm, but she gave Bronco Mallory an inquiring look. "Really, or are you joking?"

She could not believe he was serious, knowing that wild donkeys were evasive and temperamental creatures and the sport was dangerous.

Bronco laughed. "Meant what I said. Of course you might just happen to catch a gem thief while you're out in the desert. I hear one is headed that way."

"What!" cried Linda, her interest quickened.

Grandfather Thomas Mallory was a tall, firmly knit man with thick, iron-gray hair and keen blue eyes that crinkled at the edges. He had acquired the nickname of Bronco when as a small boy he often imitated the actions of the ranch's broncs.

Now he snatched off his big hat and smacked the dust from it against a knee. "Cactus Mac and some of the men have decided to go out and try to round up a bunch of little wildies. They're in great demand now. Mac thought you might like to go along."

"We sure would!" cried Linda.

Cactus Mac, the ranch foreman, had contributed much to the good times and excitement which sixteen-year-old Linda and her eighteen-year-old brother Bob had had since coming to Rancho del Sol.

Their parents had died several months previously in Hawaii, where Major Craig had been stationed. Linda and Bob had come to southern California to live with their grandparents on the big horse and cattle ranch in the San Quinto Valley. Linda revealed her Spanish ancestry with her lustrous black hair and eyes, and was the fourth generation to carry the name Rosalinda. Bob, with bright brown eyes and sandy hair, favored his father's Scottish ancestry.

"A wild donkey hunt sounds great," he said with a grin.

"And a mystery to solve makes it even better," declared Linda. "There's nothing special doing here until the Sun Val Park fair. You know I've been asked to show Chica and have her do some tricks."

Chica d'Oro was Linda's prize, trophy-winning palomino.

"We'll be back long before the fair opens," said Bronco.

Bob asked, "What do we do with the donks if we should manage to round up any? Sell them wild?"

"Not by a long sight," replied Bronco. "We'll break them to pack and to the cart."

"Chica will be a big help catching them," Linda remarked with a chuckle.

The others laughed, recalling how the filly had wandered out on the desert one night while Linda and some friends were on a trip, and had found a little stray, maltreated donkey. The two animals had become inseparable for a while. The donkey, named Vagabond, was now a pampered member of the Rancho del Sol family.

"When do we start, and what do we need for the trip?" Linda asked eagerly.

"We'll leave in the morning," Bronco replied. "Cactus and his men will take care of all the arrangements. Just be ready to ride."

"I'll be up early," said Linda. "Now tell us about the gem thief."

"I suggest," Bronco replied, "that you phone your pal Kathy and ask her. Incidentally she may want to ride with us."

Linda hurried to the house and put in the call to her good friend Kathy Hamilton, a warm honey-blonde with an apricot-glow complexion. Kathy's father owned the Highway House, which contained a restaurant and a lapidary shop where he sold semiprecious gems from the desert. He also cut and polished gems for the many rock hounds who came to the area.

Kathy was upset. "Someone broke into Dad's lapidary shop last night!" she exclaimed. "A customer's collection of garnets, which had been left for cutting and polishing, was stolen."

"How dreadful!" Linda said. "Bronco said that a gem thief escaped into the desert. Is your burglar the one he meant?"

"I guess so. Deputy Sheriff Randall found some dry chunks of reddish-gray mud that probably came off the man's shoes. He said it might have come from a place out in the high desert where they get the special mud to use in oil wells. It's near the Calico Mountain gemstone area. Horse tracks led in that direction."

"Was anything else stolen?" Linda asked.

"No."

"Then the thief must have known about the collection and wanted only the garnets," said Linda. "Are there any clues to the burglar's identity?"

"Some red hairs were found on the doorframe where that awful man must have bumped his head.

Randall said the thief was apparently tall, since he had a long stride."

"That's a good bit to go on," said Linda. "If the thief *is* out in the desert we may be able to capture him while we're there on our wild donkey round-up."

"Your what?" asked Kathy.

Linda explained and said, "Want to go along?"

Her friend was silent for several seconds but finally agreed to join the party. "It sounds horribly dangerous," she declared, "but I wouldn't miss the chance of helping to capture that red-haired thief and getting back the stolen garnets. I'll ride over to Old Sol early in the morning."

"Come for breakfast," Linda suggested.

Next she telephoned Larry Spencer at his father's saddle and leather goods shop in the nearby town of Lockwood. Larry was thrilled to go along. "I'll be over for an early start," he promised. Larry always rode an Old Sol horse, usually the brown cow pony Gypsy.

As Linda returned to the corral to tell Bronco and Bob the news, Grandmother Mallory came toward them from a paddock. She had just returned after a brisk ride. Mrs. Mallory was an expert horsewoman and had won many honors.

Linda and Bob, who affectionately called her Doña, smiled at the tall, slender woman. She wore a tan cotton blouse and brown jodhpurs. Rango, the big yellow coyote-shepherd dog, bounded along at her side.

Doña smiled warmly at the trio by the corral fence. "What plot are you three hatching?" she asked.

"Wild donkey and gem thief hunt," replied Linda. "Have you ever ridden on one?"

"I've watched a couple of donkey captures," Doña answered. "It will have all the excitement and surprises that you could wish for. And adding a manhunt to it! All I can say is, be careful!"

"You're right, Roz," said Bronco, looking at her fondly.

Roz, a nickname Bronco always called his wife, had been derived, as Linda's had, from the name of their ancestor, Rosalinda Perez. Grandmother Mallory was a beautiful woman, graceful and dignified, with lovely graying black hair twisted in a knot at the nape of her neck. Her olive skin was smooth and she had soft brown eyes.

"Everyone ready for tea or hot chocolate?" she asked, smiling. A late-afternoon snack on the patio of the large, tree-shaded adobe house was a long-established custom at the ranch.

"I'm ready for more than a snack," said Bob, grinning. "But that'll tide me over until dinnertime."

Early the following day, a typical bright August morning, Kathy arrived on Patches, her brown and white pinto. Larry drove in a few minutes after breakfast. The tall eighteen-year-old had been a summer pal of Bob's from early childhood, when the Craigs had started spending their long vacations at the ranch.

Larry looked at Bob and said, "I don't mind these girls going on a wild donkey hunt, but what's the idea of their being on a manhunt? Don't we rate any more? What's the matter with us?"

"Guess it's because we don't have red hair," Bob responded with a grin.

"Or a fortune in garnets," Larry added with a tremendous sigh of resignation.

Linda and Kathy looked at each other. Should they retort to this teasing or ignore it? They were saved the necessity of a decision by the approach of Bronco, who ordered, "Mount up, everybody!"

The four young people hurried to their horses. Linda stepped into the stirrup and pulled herself astride Chica d'Oro, whose golden coat and white-stockinged feet gleamed in the sunlight. "Good morning, baby," she said, caressing the filly.

Bob swung himself into the saddle on his quarter horse Rocket, and Larry onto the cow pony Gypsy. Cactus Mac, the bandy-legged, gray-haired foreman, would ride his buckskin, Buck, and lead the hunt. Bronco sat easily on his handsome big chestnut Morgan named Colonel.

A ranch hand went ahead in the jeep, carrying

lumber for the donkey trap, the bedrolls, and the food. A couple of other cowboys were waiting on horseback to follow.

Doña stood nearby with Luisa Alvarez, the plump Mexican housekeeper, to wave the riders on their way. Rango sat on his haunches beside them, aggrievedly beating his tail in the dust at his orders to stay home and guard the ranch.

Luisa cautioned, "*Amigos*, remember, those desert canaries you go after are little maybe, but they make weapons of their flying hooves. *Sí, Sí!*"

"We'll remember," said Linda, blowing kisses as she rode off.

The ranch hands knew where to find the donkeys. Headed by the jeep, the group rode out toward the high desert where the flat, sandy terrain gave way to arroyos and rocky buttes.

"This is certainly desolate country," said Kathy. "Why do you suppose those little jacks and jennies pick it for a home?"

Cactus Mac heard her question and answered, "Good hidin' for one thing. An' then thar's mighty good forage in the pockets 'round the rocks. Wherever thar's donks, we're sure to find water."

"If anyone sees a red-haired man hiding among the rocks, let us know," said Linda.

Suddenly she became aware that Chica was favoring a hind foot. Soon the palomino began to limp badly.

"Hold up!" Linda called out and quickly dismounted.

She lifted Chica's hoof. A small, jagged rock was wedged between the bar and frog. Linda could not budge it with her finger, so she took out the curved-end hoof-pick tool she always carried in her saddlebag.

Larry immediately came to help her and held up Chica's hoof while Linda pried out the little rock. She scrutinized it closely for a moment. The rock was of an odd, dull, reddish color instead of the usual gray or tan of desert rocks.

Kathy leaned down from her horse. "What is it?"

Linda handed up the stone.

"Well, what do you know!" exclaimed Kathy. "It's a garnet! Trust that highfalutin Chica to find it!"

"A garnet!" Linda repeated in astonishment.

"Maybe we're in a bed of them!" cried Bob, dismounting and kicking about the silty, pebbly soil.

"Not likely," said Bronco. "This is probably just one that washed in here."

"Garnet or no garnet, I hope it didn't bruise Chica's hoof," said Linda, dropping the stone into her pocket and circling Chica to check her gait.

The horse tossed her head and pranced in a pivot, relieved that her foot no longer hurt. Everyone laughed.

"Didn't you tell that nag we're on a donkey hunt,

and not a rock-hound excursion?" Bob teased.

Linda replied, "Chica may have picked up a clue to the gem thief. Remember, he likes garnets."

"That's right," said Kathy. "He may be hiding around here."

There was no sign of him, however, so Linda and Larry finally mounted and followed their companions.

At the foot of a draw, Cactus Mac held up a hand. "We'll build our trap here," he announced. "Everyone get busy and bring in some brush."

The ranch hands worked fast and in a short while had a skeleton corral thrown up. When the others fastened their mesquite branches to hide the bars, the trap looked like a desert oasis.

"Very good job," Bronco praised them. "That ought to catch some desert donks. How about our eating while we're waiting?" The bunkhouse cook had prepared big ham sandwiches, apple pie, coffee, and milk.

As soon as the Old Solers had finished the meal, Cactus Mac said, "We'll split into three groups and fan out in different directions up above thar. The first group that sights a bunch o' donks, hoot like an ole owl. The rest of you circle 'round and we'll run the wildies down the draw into this here trap.

"And watch sharp. The critters are cute 'bout doublin' back, or the lot of 'em might even go sky-hootin' through a hole. If they get away from

16

you an' hit for the rocks, let 'em go. The little beasts are sure-footed as mountain goats, but if the horses try the rocks, they'll get cut up or maybe break one o' their legs."

"I wouldn't say this is child's play," Linda remarked.

"Who's a child?" Bob asked with a grin.

"Me, maybe," Kathy admitted, blue eyes wide with apprehension.

"Stick to the draw, and you'll make out all right," Bob told her.

Bronco and the four young people formed one group. They went zigzagging up the rough side of the slope.

Kathy's eyes roved over the desert and up above her, then she said, "I don't see even one donkey."

"I think I do every once in a while," said Larry, "but it turns out to be—just Bob." His pal gave him a dark look.

Just then they heard an owl hoot coming from their left. "String out now nearer the floor until we see the donks," ordered Bronco. "Then keep a fast riding line on this side of them to prevent a breakthrough."

Suddenly they saw the little gray animals crashing down from a hidden cove. The hard-riding cowboys were giving yipee-ki-oos and yelling close behind the loudly braying animals. Linda's group kept their line, preventing the donkeys from turning up the slope and forcing them down the draw.

Surrounded, the donkeys ran a straight course and the first of the noisy, hee-hawing lot went into the trap. Others, bellowing, scattered at the entrance.

Linda rode Chica d'Oro along one side of the brush corral to turn back a jenny and her black, fuzzy, long-eared baby. They were an adorable pair, Linda thought, and suddenly wanted them for her own. She managed to turn the two and herd them along the side of the trap, then crowd the animals through the entrance. To Linda's relief, they ran to join the other confused donkeys who were at the opposite end pushing against the brush-covered bars.

Quickly Linda rode away from the entrance to clear it for any other donkeys being herded in. At this moment a big jack galloped from the far side of the trap straight toward her!

He must be maddened by Chica's unusual coloring, or perhaps he's the mate of the jenny I captured! she thought.

Linda wondered how to escape him. She pulled hard to the side. But the jack was lightning quick. He instantly whirled next to her and let fly with his razor-sharp hooves!

Strange Turquoise 2

Linda pulled back on Chica d'Oro's reins so hard and suddenly that it caused the filly to rear. This split-second move saved the palomino from the donkey's vicious, sharp hooves, which had slashed through the air dangerously close to the horse's chest.

As soon as Chica came down, Linda turned her toward the trap on a run. The jack followed. But before he could whirl and kick, Larry's rope encircled the animal and pulled him hard to the ground on his side.

"Let that critter go!" Cactus shouted. "He's a mean 'un."

Larry loosened his rope, and smacked it across the cantankerous jack's rump. As the animal went scooting upward among the rocks, Linda dismounted and stood quietly for a few moments, breathing deeply to regain her composure.

"Are you all right?" asked Larry, riding over to her.

She smiled. "I am now. Thanks for rescuing me."

Bob joined them and said, "That donk must be king of the herd! He's ready to fight for the others in spite of the odds against him."

Chica d'Oro, considerably upset, was pawing and sweating profusely. Linda fondled the filly's head. "I'll fix you up right now, baby. We're thankful you didn't get hurt by that tough little rascal."

She led the palomino over to a spot partially shaded by mesquite, removed the bridle and saddle, and rubbed the horse down with a piece of sacking. Then she tethered Chica and gave her a treat of carrot chunks from the saddlebag.

I'll bet that jenny and her baby would like some carrots too, thought Linda, and took two handfuls of them over to the corral trap.

The entrance had been strongly barred, and the Old Sol hunters stood around looking over the haul. There were five donkeys besides the jenny and her colt.

One of the men had thrown them some alfalfa which had been brought on the jeep. The animals were attacking the succulent green hay ravenously.

"I'm sure that tastes heavenly to them after the bits of tough old dry stuff they find around these rocks," said Kathy.

"At least it keeps them quiet," Linda added.

She walked around the enclosure and approached as close as possible to the jenny and her baby without alarming them. She stretched out a handful of carrots.

The jenny regarded the offer suspiciously, so Linda dropped the pieces to the ground. At once the colt dashed forward and picked up a morsel with his eager gray lips. His mother quickly followed him and scooped the rest into her mouth. After tasting the carrots, she suddenly thrust her nose into the girl's hand. Linda laughed and fed the jenny and her son the remaining chunks, then ran for her camera.

Upon her return she decided it would be safe for her to go inside the enclosure. Approaching the jenny she said, "I'm going to take your picture. Hold still!"

Instead of obeying, the donkey ran to Linda and thrust an eager nose at the camera, probably in search of more carrot bits.

"She doesn't think she's photogenic enough for a picture," called Kathy, giggling.

Everyone laughed as Linda kept moving backward to get far enough away from the gray beast to take a snap. The donkey was now her close friend, braying contentedly and staying as near the girl as she could.

Larry remarked in a drawl, "Wal, what d'you know! The desert canary's got a song only for Lindy Craig!"

"That jenny and her colt," said Bronco, "are a good pair. You did a mighty fine job, Linda, riding them into the trap."

Just then a voice rang out, "Come and get it!"

The jeep driver, who was cook for the trip, was calling everyone to supper. He had driven two forked sticks into the ground and laid a tough mesquite bar across them. Hanging on the bar over a fire of glowing coals was a huge iron kettle of stew and a big pot of coffee. Beside the fire stood another iron kettle full of sourdough biscuits. On the open tailgate of the jeep were cans of peaches ready to be spooned out.

"Boy, does this chow taste good!" exclaimed Bob, going for a second helping.

When everyone had finished eating, Cactus Mac announced with a grin, "Lookee thar! We got strangers in camp."

The others turned and followed the foreman's gaze. A little distance away two large, armor-plated desert tortoises were approaching each other.

"Are they going to fight?" Kathy gasped.

"They can't do no more'n bump each other around some," replied Mac with a laugh.

The two bony-shelled creatures moved forward

cautiously and touched noses. They pressed them together for a full minute while the watchers held their breaths. One tortoise finally pulled away and circled around the other. Both of them, obviously satisfied that they were in good company, moved off side by side to seek the shelter of some nearby mesquite bush or a rock crevice.

"Not a very exciting romance," Kathy whispered to Linda, who laughed.

The cowboys took the horses up to the donkeys' water hole for a drink, and brought back full buckets for the corralled animals.

By this time the kettles had been removed from the crossbar, and the fire built up. For the next half hour the cowboys entertained the others with songs and tall tales. Then "sack down" time was called by Cactus Mac.

Before crawling into her bedroll, Linda took the garnet from her pocket and held it before the flames. It still appeared dull. She sighed. "I don't see why any rock hound would get excited about this."

Kathy replied promptly, "Ferreting out the hidden beauty in all these desert mineral rocks is what's exciting. It's thrilling to discover a new location for gemstones or a new crystallite in an old location. But like all things, it takes some know-how to get the best results and most enjoyment."

Bronco smiled. "I'm thinking, young lady, that you've acquired a good bit of that lecture working with your dad."

"You're right," Kathy admitted. "I can recognize most varieties now. Often stones that look drab and uninteresting in the daylight are absolutely magnificent under ultraviolet light. Dad showed me a piece of willemite and calcite that looked like an ordinary dark stone with a light streak through it. But under an ultraviolet lamp, the dark part was brilliant green and the streak was bright red."

"I'm fast becoming a rock hound," said Bob. "Think I'll get one of those ultraviolet lanterns and start out."

"You may be sorry," said Kathy with an impish grin. "The soft, bright glow from a fluorescent object is a little spooky. You might even find when you stoop over to examine one of those glowing spots that you've flushed a scorpion! They fluoresce vividly as long as they're in the ultraviolet light."

"That wouldn't stop Brave Bob," Larry spoke up, then added seriously, "I suppose the rock hounds that bring their finds for your dad to cut and polish have plenty of adventures to tell about."

Kathy laughed. "Oh, sure. They're pretty much the same, but each one thinks his was the most dangerous."

"Tell us one," urged Bob.

Kathy was silent for a couple of moments. Then

she smiled and said, "There was a uranium prospector who never had any luck with his Geiger counter. Then he learned that some of the minerals containing uranium fluoresce. With new hope, he bought an ultraviolet lamp and took his wife and little girl out on a prospecting trip. He searched and searched but got no reaction with his light to indicate uranium.

"His daughter used to wander around with him, but one day the poor little kid got lost. Her mother went into a state of collapse and the father had to take his wife to a hospital. He declared that he would neither sleep nor eat until he found his little girl.

"He and a lot of other people hunted day and night without any luck. On the third night he was about to drop from exhaustion. Suddenly his ultraviolet lantern picked up a little glow. It was from a wulfenite crystal. A step farther on there was another, then another. Finally the line of them led him to his child!

"She was lying under a bush unconscious from exposure, hunger, and thirst. He took her to the hospital, too. In a short time the whole family recovered.

"The little girl had picked up a pocketful of the pretty yellow stones. When she became lost she had dropped them in a line hoping her father would follow them and find her. He had passed near this spot around noontime but wulfenite pebbles don't fluoresce in daylight, so he hadn't noticed them.

"Then her father discovered that the yellow wulfenite stones were uranium mineral. He went back to the spot and found a uranium deposit. It wasn't a large one, but it brought a good price."

"Do you ever see the man anymore?" asked Linda. "Or the little girl?"

Kathy grinned. "Oh, sure. I'm stuck with her. The sale of the uranium bought the Highway House."

"You!" cried Bob.

Kathy laughed. "The same poor little dumb kid." Linda hugged her friend, then the two girls crawled into their bedrolls.

Early the next morning Bronco, Cactus, and the four young people mounted up to return home. The ranch hand who had driven the jeep and the other two riders would remain for a couple of days to care for the donkeys and break them.

"Be good to my pets," Linda said to the camp cook. "Feed them well."

The cook grinned. "Why sure, just so long as I don't have to be a carrot-feedin' baby-sitter to that jenny!"

As the riders galloped off, Linda remarked, "We didn't catch even one glimpse of a red-haired man. I feel as if our mission in the desert was only half-accomplished."

"He wouldn't be likely to let us see him," said Bob.

"No, but he might have left some clue," Linda answered.

"You're not giving up hope he'll be found, are you?" Bronco asked.

"Oh, no," Linda assured him. "As soon as the Sun Val Park show is over, I'll do some more sleuthing for that gem thief!"

When the riders reached Kathy's home trail she said to Linda, "Bring your garnet over soon for Dad to cut and polish. He'll be glad to do it."

Linda laughed. "Thanks, Kathy. I'll come as soon as I have a chance."

The following day Linda started working Chica d'Oro in earnest for her act at the Sun Val Park fair. She took the horse around the ring a few times in her easy walk, trot, and canter gaits.

Finally, pressing gently with her calves, Linda directed the filly into the exaggerated high rack of the Spanish Walk for which she had been training the palomino for several weeks. Chica did not respond immediately or smoothly.

"But at least you understand the signal," said Linda, and patted the horse's neck. "You're doing all right, baby. It will just take a lot of practice to go into perfect performance."

She dismounted and put Chica d'Oro through her regular tricks of nodding and shaking her head yes and no, giving a horse laugh, and taking a bow. Linda had rehearsed her mount in them so often that they had become automatic with the filly.

"Now you're going to learn a new trick," Linda told her with a smile, "just for a little extra showmanship. After all, this will be the first time we'll be presented as an act, and we want to give people their money's worth!" Chica d'Oro seemed to understand. She raised her upper lip in a grin.

Linda brought over a keg and a long training whip from the side of the ring.

"Now," she said, "put your forefeet on the keg."

Chica eyed the little barrel sideways and sniffed it suspiciously. She gave the keg a sharp tap with one hoof, knocking it over.

Linda laughed. "That's hardly what I meant."

She straightened the keg, and touched each of Chica's pasterns with the whip.

"Up!" she commanded.

The palomino raised her forefeet slightly. Immediately Linda repeated the touch and word, and this time as the filly picked up her feet, Linda quickly placed one, then the other on the keg.

"Stand!" she ordered.

Chica, surprised, stood for a moment before removing her feet.

"Good!" Linda praised her, and gave the filly a chunk of carrot.

The young trainer repeated her instructions several times until at the commands "Up" and "Stand" Chica quickly placed her forefeet on the keg. With each performance, she would stand with her head up proudly and her eyes glowing with the sense of accomplishment.

"Now will you bow?" Linda asked before letting the filly down, and gave her the signal.

Chica d'Oro executed the dip of her head and pull-back of her bent right leg without difficulty as her other forefoot remained firmly atop the keg.

"Wonderful! What a beautiful finale!" Linda gave Chica the last bit of carrot, then led the palomino back to her stall for a special lunch of molasses and grain pellets.

Later that day Linda and Bob rode over to the Highway House with the dull red gemstone. They found Kathy in her father's shop classifying some raw specimens and listing them in a record book.

"Hi!" she called.

Sam Hamilton, a tall man with handsome features, looked up from his cutting wheel and smiled. "Hello there."

"Any news yet of the gem thief?" Linda asked him.

"I'm afraid not. When the owner of the stolen garnets finds out, I know he will be mighty upset. To a rock hound nothing—not even insurance money—can replace a pet collection."

"I can see why," said Linda thoughtfully. She held out her own little stone.

Mr. Hamilton examined it closely and said, "Very nice. How would you like to watch me cut and polish it right now?"

Linda's eyes glowed. "Oh, would you?"

"What shape do you prefer?"

"I—I really don't know. What do you suggest?"

"Depends on how you want it set—in a ring, pin, or—would you like to wear the gem as a captured garnet?"

"You mean in a bubble of glass on a chain?"

Mr. Hamilton nodded, his eyes twinkling.

"Say, that would be like building a ship in a bottle!" exclaimed Bob.

"Not quite," said Mr. Hamilton. "A bubble of glass is blown around the stone by a glassblower. I have such a friend in Los Angeles, and could take the garnet to him the next time I go to the city for supplies—provided you would like that, Linda."

"I'd love it," she replied.

"I'll give the stone an oval shape then," declared Mr. Hamilton, turning toward a grinding wheel.

He first cemented the stone to a dop stick, which he set into one of a series of holes on a supporting block. Next Mr. Hamilton held the stone against the revolving wheel and started grinding. By changing the dop from one hole to another, he controlled the angles of the facets he wished to make.

When the stone had acquired the proper shape, he brought it to a high polish on a cloth-covered wheel, using a fine abrasive he said was rouge powder. In a few moments he laid the gem in Linda's hand.

"It's—it's beautiful!" she cried enthusiastically.

The garnet scintillated with the candescence of its own inner fire.

Linda returned it to Mr. Hamilton. "I can hardly wait until my prize is captured in that bubble of glass."

"And I can hardly wait," Bob spoke up, "until I get one of those ultraviolet lights. I want to go rock-hounding and see what unusual specimens I can find."

Kathy laughed. "Another rock hound is born!" she teased.

"Let me show you a really unusual specimen," said Mr. Hamilton, taking a small flannel pouch from a desk drawer. Gently he dropped an opaque, green, six-sided stone from it onto a chamois square.

"It's lovely," said Linda.

"A turquoise."

Bob looked puzzled. "I thought all turquoises were blue."

"Not always," replied Mr. Hamilton. "The color ranges from blue and blue-green to blue-gray. When a blue stone is exposed to excessive sunlight or heat it becomes dehydrated and turns green."

"Where did this one come from?" asked Linda.

"Charlie Tonka, your old Indian friend who lives out near Fossil Mountain, brought it in to me. He was upset over its turning green."

"Charlie Tonka!" exclaimed Linda. An affectionate recollection of him raced through her mind. Chica d'Oro had been given to her by the Indian in exchange for two ranch horses. He had found the filly's Arabian mother injured in the desert and taken her home not long before she had foaled.

Two customers, one tall, the other of medium height, had come into the shop. They stepped closer to the group and listened attentively.

Mr. Hamilton, wary since the theft of the garnets, dropped a cloth over the odd green turquoise. "Is there something I can do for you?" he asked the men.

"Yes," answered the tall man, who had a beaklike nose and thin lips. "I'm Ralph Fallon, and this is my partner George Hill. We own the gem shop near the entrance to Sun Val Park. We've brought three pieces of jade we'd like to have sized evenly and polished."

Mr. Hamilton took the jade and went to the polishing wheel.

"That must be a very valuable turquoise you have under the cloth," said Fallon.

Mr. Hamilton did not look up. "Fair."

"Is much turquoise found around here?" asked Hill, a dark-haired man with a straight nose and thick lips.

"Average amount," was the noncommittal answer.

After Mr. Hamilton finished the polishing job, Fallon paid him and the men left. Kathy's father uncovered the green turquoise. "This is truly a fine specimen," he said. "I believe it is actually a Persian stone. As you know, Persia is now called Iran, and that is where the deposits of the finest turquoise are located."

"Did Charlie tell you where he got this?" asked Bob.

"The Indian said he had received it from his father a long time ago. He thought it had come from the Shadow Mountains where old Indian tribes had discovered deposits of turquoise many years before." Mr. Hamilton held up the gem. "But I feel sure that this is a Persian stone."

"Where would Charlie's father have gotten it?" asked Linda, puzzled.

"Possibly from some international mineralogist who had come to check on the Shadow Mountain deposits."

"I can see I'll need more know-how to become a

rock hound," said Bob, looking through the collection of books that Mr. Hamilton had for sale.

He bought a U.S. Geological Survey listing locations where gemstone minerals might be found, and another book with illustrations describing in detail the various types of gemstones. Then he and Linda thanked the lapidary, said good-bye to him and Kathy, and left for Old Sol.

After breakfast the next morning, Linda rehearsed Chica again in the Spanish Walk. This time the palomino responded much more smoothly, and by the end of the practice session Linda felt greatly encouraged. Just then Doña called her to the telephone.

Linda said "Hello," and Kathy's excited voice came over the wire.

"The Persian turquoise has been stolen!"

Mysterious Ambush 3

Linda was shocked speechless for a moment at this startling news of a second gem theft. She asked Kathy, "How did the thief break in?"

"Exactly the way the first did," Kathy replied. "By breaking the latch on a back window. Dad thinks the same person was here twice, because we found a few red hairs on the desk where the turquoise was kept. And there was a little more of that grayish-red mud by the door."

"Could they by any chance have been left the first time and overlooked?"

"No, they couldn't have. The place was cleaned thoroughly."

"Have you notified the sheriff?" Linda asked.

"Yes, and Deputy Sheriff Randall came at once. After looking over the shop, he went into town to check on anyone who might have been out in the area where the odd mud is found. He said that the trucker who hauls and sells the mud to the oil companies might be able to tell him who else has been out there.

"In the meantime," Kathy went on, "I wish you and Bob would ride over and look around. You may discover something that the rest of us have missed."

"Thanks for the compliment," said Linda. "We'll be right over!"

She returned to the others and told them of the Hamiltons' second burglary. "Kathy would like Bob and me to do some sleuthing in the shop. Okay, Bob?"

"You bet. And here comes Larry. He has some leather equipment his dad mended for Cactus. We'll take him along."

Linda and Bob joined Larry on the patio, and the three drove in his jeep to the Highway House. They systematically went over the lapidary shop, but did not find a single new clue.

Mr. Hamilton, usually vigorous and alert, sat slumped in the desk chair, his sensitive, artistic fingers strumming idly on the walnut desktop. His expression was troubled. "The thief isn't a rock hound, I'm sure, because rock hounds just aren't thieves. The thrill of discovery, not burglary, is the thing that gives them their constant incentive to obtain gems."

"Who's been in here besides rock-hound customers?" asked Larry.

Mr. Hamilton shrugged. "No one else is interested in browsing around."

Linda wondered about this. Aloud she said, "Someone must have learned about your most valuable specimens, and is making a collection of them for a purpose," she deduced. "Probably he'll sell them."

"Let's take a look outdoors for clues," Bob suggested.

The others followed him and examined the various windowsills and the ground beneath them.

"Here's something!" cried Bob.

He had been searching at a little distance from the others, who hurried to his side. He pointed to horseshoe prints and some of the peculiar red-gray mud.

Kathy said excitedly, "That mud must have fallen out of the hooves of the thief's horse!"

Linda did not agree with this theory. "That isn't likely on loose soil. When a horse walks on pavement any dry mud on the sole of its foot will knock off, but not in a soft, earthy spot like this."

"Maybe the rider cleaned his horse's hooves out here," Larry suggested.

Linda had been bending over to scrutinize the horseshoe prints closely. "Do you know what I think—there wasn't any horse here at all! Look at the way those shoes are turned. No horse ever steps like that. I think someone hand-pressed horseshoes into the silt to make those prints, and deliberately dropped the mud here."

She stood up and looked thoughtfully at the others. "And those red hairs—they could have been placed by the thief just where they were seen."

The others were dumbfounded. "To throw suspicion on someone else?" Larry asked.

"Either that, or simply to divert attention from himself."

"That means," Bob said, "the burglar could be a local person since he seems so familiar with Mr. Hamilton's valuable specimens."

"A professional jewel thief nearby!" Kathy exclaimed. "And we can't even guess at his identity! Oh, it gives me the shivers just to think he may be right around here!"

"We'd better get busy and find him!" said Bob.

"But how do we know whom to look for if the thief doesn't have red hair?" asked Kathy.

"There's bound to be a break soon," Linda prophesied optimistically.

Kathy looked worried. "The Sun Val Park committee members are counting on my father's having a booth at the fair. They thought it would be one of the main attractions. Dad figured he might make a lot of sales, but with this thief loose I suppose it wouldn't be safe for him to have his collection on display."

"Sure it will be," said Bob. "We'll all stand by to keep an eye on the booth."

Early on opening day of the fair, Mr. Hamilton went to the park to put the finishing touches on his booth. Mrs. Hamilton and Kathy planned to drive over with the boxed gemstone exhibits and certain articles to sell. They were to arrive in time to display them by nine-thirty, when the gates would open to the public.

Kathy and her youthful-looking mother usually seemed more like sisters, but today Mrs. Hamilton appeared frail and older. The thefts in the lapidary shop had made her very nervous.

Kathy noted her mother's paleness and asked gently, "You don't feel like going to the park this morning, do you?"

"I really don't," sighed Mrs. Hamilton.

"Please go back to bed," said Kathy. "I can load the boxes and get them to the booth alone." She accompanied her mother into their house and made her lie down.

Kathy had just returned to the shop when Bob came in. "Thought I'd see if I could lend you and your mother a hand," he said.

"I never was so glad to see anyone in my life," Kathy declared, and gave him a bright smile. "You can lend me two hands! Mother is ill, and I'm on my own."

Bob picked up one of the many heavy boxes. "I'll load these into my station wagon and we'll whisk over to the park in a jiffy."

Back at Rancho del Sol, Linda was ready to leave. Chica d'Oro was standing in her trailer. Bronco took the wheel of the car and, with Doña and Linda beside him, drove to the park. Chica's first exhibition was not scheduled until eleven, but Linda knew the horse would perform better if given a little time to become acquainted with her strange surroundings. The filly would go on again at two and four in the afternoon, and seven and nine in the evening.

All the acts at the fair were to be given on the Little League ball field where there was a circle of bleachers. Linda found a cool spot for Chica under the shade of a blooming blue jacaranda tree.

"Just relax, baby," she said, preparing to leave. "I won't be gone long."

She and the Mallorys walked over to the booth section to see the Hamilton array of gemstones. The lapidary stood there alone, looking worried. "Kathy and her mother were to have been here long before this," he said.

"I'm sure they'll come soon," said Linda, but wondered what had happened.

Meanwhile Kathy had helped Bob load the mineral rocks and gemstones into the station wagon and started for the park. As they went along a chaparral-fringed road, Kathy suddenly laid a hand on Bob's arm.

"Look there! Isn't that a man lying along the side of the road?"

Bob slowed, straining his eyes ahead. "It certainly is. He's not moving! Maybe he was struck by a hit-and-run driver!"

Bob stopped the car quickly. They got out and hurried to the figure.

"It's a dummy!" Bob cried in surprise.

"Could be someone's scarecrow that pranksters stole and dumped here," suggested Kathy. "Why don't we—"

She was interrupted by a harsh voice behind her. "Get back in the car and don't put up an argument or you'll be sorry!"

Kathy and Bob wheeled to face two masked men!

"What's this all about?" Bob asked as the intruders moved toward the car. His jaw was set and he had a white line of anger around his lips, but resistance at this moment seemed too dangerous to be undertaken. The men made no answer.

"The gemstone thieves!" murmured Kathy to Bob when they were in the front seat of the car. "Here go all of Dad's most valuable specimens!"

The two strangers kicked the dummy out of sight behind a bush and climbed into the back seat. One said, "Turn to the right off the road, boy, and keep driving until I tell you to stop."

Bob was sure he could not proceed very far on this road without getting stuck in the sand, but there seemed to be enough silt mixed with it for traction. He drove a long way into the desert.

Finally one of the men said, "Stop here." He reached over the front seat and snatched the ignition key. Then he and his companion jumped out and hurriedly walked away, disappearing behind a huge clump of mesquite.

"Well, of all the crazy things!" exclaimed Kathy, when they were out of hearing range. "They didn't even take a look at Dad's packages."

"I'm glad I didn't give in to my impulse to fight them," said Bob. "Maybe they're not the gemstone thieves, but just a couple of outlaws who wanted a ride into the desert. Anyhow, we're safe. I was afraid they had guns. That's why I didn't tangle with them."

"Why did they take the car key?" Kathy asked.

"To prevent us from getting back and notifying the authorities before they manage to locate a safe hideaway."

"How will we ever get back now?" Kathy wailed.

The sound of a helicopter overhead drew their attention. It appeared to be coming down.

"This could be a way out of here," said Bob hopefully.

"Dad must have sent a search copter after us when we failed to arrive at the park on time," Kathy said, brightening.

When the helicopter settled on the desert, she jumped from the car with Bob and ran to it. Simultaneously the two masked men stepped from their brush shield and one commanded: "Back, you two! This is for us!"

Kathy and Bob looked in desperation at the pilot, only to find he had a handkerchief tied over his face! Another outlaw! The two waiting men climbed into the helicopter and it started to rise.

Bob wrote down the number, then looked thoughtfully at Kathy. "Did you notice the big, odd-looking ring one of those men was wearing—a brown square with wavy dark lines through it?"

"Yes, I did," said Kathy. "It looked like petrified wood. And now I know where I saw it once before. One of those two men from the gem shop who brought the jade in for Dad to polish had on a ring like that! I noticed it because the color is unusual. It happens to be a rare species of dark brown agate."

"Well, that gives us a good clue to the identity of one of our captors," said Bob.

"But not an answer on how to get out of here," said Kathy woefully. "This is a very dangerous place to be stranded—snakes, scorpions, poisonous insects, heat, and no water!"

And, Bob thought, we wouldn't last long trying to walk to the road in this heat.

"Oh, Bob," cried Kathy, "what are we going to do?"

A Suspicious Confession   4

Bob gave Kathy a knowing look. "Cheer up. I've tinkered with cars since I was a kid." He reached into the glove compartment and brought out what appeared to be a large jackknife.

"Are you going to start it with one of those blades?"

Bob grinned. "Sort of, only different." He pulled out the gadgets inside the knife case, showing Kathy a big blade, bottle opener, fork, spoon, and a tiny pair of pliers. "I've been carrying this contraption for a long time, and never before had any occasion like this to use it."

He flipped all the attachments back into place except the blade and the pliers. Then he opened the car hood.

"Kathy, climb into the driver's seat and when I

tell you, step on the accelerator. Meanwhile, if you see anyone, yell."

"That will be a pleasure," said Kathy with a wry grin as she took her position. She kept a roving gaze on the desert, while watching Bob with wide-eyed interest.

He cut the wire to the coil, bypassing the switch, attached it to the battery wire, and firmly clamped it on with the pliers. The motor coughed.

"Give her gas!" Bob yelled, and Kathy pushed down on the accelerator. The engine caught at once.

Bob quickly closed the hood. "Slide over, but don't take your foot off the accelerator till I can get mine there."

"You're a wonder." Kathy sighed happily.

He climbed in beside her, put his foot on the pedal, and commenced driving carefully back to the road. As soon as he reached it, Bob speeded up and headed for the park.

"One of those kidnappers apparently is a gem shop owner—and a thief," said Kathy. "But why do you suppose he wanted to keep us away from the park with Dad's exhibits?"

"We're going to find out—and very soon!" Bob declared grimly.

When they drove up to the back of the Hamilton booth, the couple were greeted with much relief and a lot of questioning by Kathy's father, Doña,

Bronco, Linda, Larry, and a park officer. Bob hastily explained what had happened, mentioning the brown stone ring worn by one of the abductors. "It appeared to be identical with a ring we saw on Ralph Fallon, one of the gem shop owners."

"I'll look for him," the officer promised.

Everyone was mystified as to the exact reason for the kidnapping. They discussed it freely while helping Mr. Hamilton place his exhibits in the booth to make an artistic display.

Passersby who had looked at the empty booth with curiosity now paused to gaze with interest. They questioned Mr. Hamilton about the specimens, and several people bought from the collection of polished stones ready for setting.

Meanwhile, Bob went to the park office to telephone the sheriff. He reported the abduction and gave the number of the helicopter.

To Bob's surprise the desk officer said, "We had an earlier report on that helicopter from Larchmont Field advising us that it had been stolen. We have just received word from a search plane that the copter was discovered abandoned on Gopher Flats out in the desert."

"Then there's no telling where those men are," said Bob.

"Not yet, but the search is still on."

While Bob was gone, Linda, who had a little time before her first performance with Chica, hurried over to the gem shop near the entrance gate. As she went in the front door, Fallon came from the back room. Linda noticed at once the square brown agate ring that he wore.

"What is it you're looking for?" he asked. He seemed nervous and out of breath as if he had just hurried in.

"I'm only browsing." She smiled. "I'll be back later."

Linda ran to the Hamilton booth, and quickly whispered to Bob, "Fallon has returned to the gem shop! I saw a brown agate ring on his finger!"

"I want to talk to him," said Bob with determination.

He and Linda hurried to the gem shop. When Fallon saw Bob, the color drained from his face.

"You didn't expect us to meet again so soon, did you?" Linda's brother snapped.

"Don't know what you're talking about," said Fallon in an attempt at bravado.

"You know all right!" said Bob. "There is no other agate ring like the one you're wearing. You had it on when you kidnapped Kathy Hamilton and myself. That's evidence enough against you for the police."

"Police! Oh, come now," said Fallon, "this isn't worth bringing in the police. All right, I'll admit I was one of the men who forced you to drive into the desert. But I was compelled to do it by someone else and no harm came to you." He looked dolefully at the Craigs. "I must warn you I have a real bad heart, and it likely wouldn't stand a strain, and for no good reason."

Linda whispered an aside to Bob: "We don't want anything to happen to him before he talks."

Bob said to Fallon, "Explain then why you abandoned Kathy, me, and Mr. Hamilton's fair exhibits out there in the desert."

Fallon ran his tongue over his thin lips. "My partner and I have just gotten started here in the gem shop. When we heard that Hamilton was going to have a mineral rock booth at the fair, we calculated he'd take all our business away. If crowds of people bought stones from him, they wouldn't even come to our shop."

A sudden glitter came into his eyes, and he twisted his lips wryly. "You'd better not squeal to the police. I've got partners who wouldn't like that, and both of you would be in danger from them."

More threats! thought Linda. And I'll bet his heart is okay. Aloud she asked Fallon, "Do you sometimes go rock hunting out by Calico Mountain?"

She knew that was where the gray-red mud came from, and she hoped to trap him into a statement that would tie him in with that clue.

But he answered, "Never been there."

Bob stated flatly, "Kidnapping is a criminal offense."

The wheedling tone returned to Fallon's voice. "All we wanted to do was keep the exhibit from the fair. We meant no harm to you and your girl friend, young fellow. We were going to let someone know later where you were."

Linda had glanced at her wristwatch. Worriedly she said, "Bob, I must go at once and dress for my first performance."

"I'll go with you," Bob offered. "See you again, Mr. Fallon."

On their way Linda said, "There was hardly any stock in that shop. Maybe it's only a front for some illegal activities—like stealing gems to sell for a big price."

"You're probably right, Linda. But if we string Fallon along for a while we or the police may be able to find out who his partners are."

"And catch them with some stolen goods," Linda added.

When she returned to Chica, Larry was standing beside the filly, who nickered a soft greeting. "Hi, baby! Hi, Larry!" Linda hugged and petted the gleaming golden palomino.

"Oh, to live a horse's life!" muttered Larry, and Linda wrinkled her nose at him.

"Chica was beginning to think she would have to perform without you," he teased.

"She almost could," said Linda, as she glanced toward the ball field.

The bleachers were full and crowds stood around. The first act had started—an elaborate drill by Boy Scouts. It was to be followed in order by baton twirlers, a dog act, a magician, Linda and Chica, and a Mexican orchestra with singers and dancers.

Linda hastily told Larry what Mr. Fallon had said.

"I don't believe a word of it," he remarked scornfully, then added, "I'll saddle Chica while you change."

"Thank you, Larry. What would Chica and I do without you?"

She hurried off to dress in her bright green western-style suit with white leather fringe trimming and jewel decoration. She pulled on white boots and a white felt hat.

"You're a picture! A real doll!" Larry complimented her when she returned. "Good luck!"

Linda and Chica d'Oro, in her shining silver equipment, stood waiting for several minutes. Larry held the keg by his side, ready to bring in for the finale of their act.

When Linda was announced, she rode in and went around the ring a couple of times showing off her horse's gaits. There was enthusiastic applause. She saw Doña, Bronco, Bob, and Kathy on a front bleacher seat and acknowledged their presence with a little nod and smile.

In a moment Linda gave the signal to the man handling the record player to start her music. She put Chica into the showy Spanish Walk. The clapping was thunderous and many camera fans who lined the field snapped pictures.

Linda guided Chica d'Oro to the center of the field. The palomino bowed first to one side, then the other.

Now the young rider dismounted and asked the filly, "Do you like performing at this fair?" At Linda's signal, Chica nodded her head yes.

"Do you want to go home?" Linda asked her. And at Linda's signal her palomino shook her head no.

Fascinated children in the audience jumped up and down, crying, "More! More!"

Linda kept to her planned routine, since Chica had several performances yet to do.

She asked the horse one final question, "Does it make you happy that the children like you?" And Chica responded with a perfect horse laugh.

Everyone in the stands grinned and youngsters whistled their approval.

Larry brought in the keg. "Up!" said Linda softly to Chica. The filly daintily put her two front feet on the keg. "Stand!" commanded Linda, as she herself took a bow.

Exclamations came from the crowd along with their applause.

"Isn't she beautiful!"

"Doesn't she handle that horse magnificently!"

Linda, blushing slightly, gave Chica her signal to

bow, and the clapping, which had not stopped, was doubled in enthusiasm. When the palomino took her feet from the keg, Linda mounted again, facing the crowd on the other side of the circle, and had Chica bow once more. From the spectator response, it proved a grand finale to the act. As Linda rode Chica to the exit, Larry ran in and picked up the keg.

Kathy and Bob met her at the trailer, and Kathy hugged her friend. "You and Chica were perfectly marvelous! A park officer stayed with Dad so we could see your act. Bob and I will run the booth so Dad can take in your next performance. I heard people say that they were going to watch it again because they liked the first show so much."

That pleased Linda for it meant more money would be turned over to the camp fund for under-privileged children. This charity was to receive the largest percentage of the day's receipts.

After the Mexican act, Doña and Bronco joined the others. They congratulated Linda, then Bronco said, "Chow time! Follow me!"

They went to the big pit barbecue which was sending its tantalizing odors around the park. Long tables were filled with diners. It was an intriguing sight to see the big bundles of beef brought up from the pit, opened on large aluminum trays, and cut into generous slices. Besides the meat the barbe-cue included beans, slaw, bread, coffee, and milk.

An adjoining church booth sold pie and cake.

"Listen!" commanded Bob suddenly.

A member of the committee was walking about calling out, "Gold panning contest! Keep your gold and win a prize!"

"This is where I get rich quick!" exclaimed Bob.

Bronco snorted. "What does a young tenderfoot like you know about panning gold?"

"I've seen it done a lot in the movies," replied Bob. "All you do is shake a pan of pay dirt in running water. The dirt washes away, leaving the particles of gold in the bottom of the pan."

Bronco gave his grandson a sharp look under half-closed lids. "Seeing it done and doing it are two different things."

"Have you ever panned?" asked Linda.

"Many a time," replied Bronco. Laughing, he said with an old-timer's drawl, "Bought vittles with my dust more'n once when I was a young fiddle-foot sprig." The others laughed.

Bob asked, "How about you and me having a little private competition between us while we're in the concession contest? The loser has to shine the other's boots."

"I'll take you on for that one," replied Bronco.

"Is there pay dirt at the park creek?" asked Linda, amazed.

"There is now," said Larry. "The committee brought in a load from Yellow Hawk Gold Mine out in Thunder Mountain. Contestants pay a quarter for a pan."

"It's really just for fun, and an attraction for the Sun Val Park fair crowd," said Doña.

At two o'clock, Bronco and Bob stood near the creek with their pans. There was a long line of contestants. When the signal was given to start, each one bent down to the running water and dipped his pan into it.

"You can certainly tell who has done this before, and who hasn't," commented a watcher, as Bob filled his pan with water and gravel and shook it vigorously.

"Will you look at that fellow in the big hat?" said another. "He really has the knack. Tom Mallory, isn't it?"

More and more watchers gathered around Bronco. He kept his pan tipped, and let in just a little water at a time, gradually washing out small amounts of dirt.

A woman who was gazing at Bronco cried out, "I see gold there in your pan!"

Mr. Mallory's eyes crinkled at the edges. He opened the little bottle that had been provided him, and dropped in the tiny speck of gold. Then he returned to his slow, easy, methodical washing.

Bob shook his own pan all the more vigorously, let in more running water, and slopped out a good portion of possible pay dirt into the creek.

"I'm going to find some gold!" he cried, reaching far out and trying to scoop his pan full from the bottom of the creek. The rock on which Bob was crouching tipped and he landed facedown in the creek! The crowd whooped and laughed.

Bob quickly pulled back, wet to the waist in front. He grinned good-naturedly, waving his empty pan.

There were three minutes yet to go in the concession contest. Bronco kept at his washing.

"Time's up!" came the order finally, and the contestants stopped.

Bronco's pan had by far the best showing. There were several gold particles in the bottle and a little pile at the side of his pan with all the dirt washed away.

Four other contestants, like Bob, had a few specks showing, but dirt still remained in their pans.

"The winner!" called out the judge, putting a hand on Bronco's shoulder. "And a real pay dirt prospector if I've ever seen one."

He presented Grandfather Mallory with an old-time statuette of miners. The other four were presented with small pickax mementos.

As Bronco put the rest of his gold bits into the little bottle and dropped it into his pocket along with the prize, he whispered to Bob, "Any more contests you want to enter against me?"

His grandson grinned. "Guess I'll have to shine your boots," he said.

Linda had missed the gold panning fun due to her afternoon performances. She had spent the intervening time at the ball field caring for Chica and talking to people about the horse.

Larry had stayed with her until late afternoon. Then, since he had to return home to make a delivery for his father, he offered to take Doña and Bronco home. They accepted.

"It has been a splendid day," said Doña. "You rode superbly, Linda, and to think your grandfather is the champion gold panner!"

Bob stayed to help Linda during the evening performances. At the proper moments he brought in the keg. At each performance the applause for Linda and Chica was deafening.

"Great work, Sis," said Bob proudly.

When the fair closed at ten o'clock, the Hamiltons took the Old Sol station wagon home with the gemstone collection and the small amount of unsold stock. The lapidary was very pleased with his day's receipts, which were high.

Bob and Linda rode toward Rancho del Sol, hauling Chica d'Oro in her special trailer.

Presently Linda said, "I've thought a lot about Mr. Fallon. Now that we know he was involved with the pilot of the stolen copter, and we suspect he was one of the Hamiltons' gem thieves, I believe we should tell this to the police."

"You're right," said Bob, "but let's wait until morning."

Linda, too weary to argue, agreed, but early the next day she and her brother set off for Lockwood. On the way to Randall's office they passed the gem shop.

"Stop!" cried Linda. "I see a sign on the door."

She jumped from the car and hurried to read the placard. It said:

CLOSED FOR ONE WEEK.
GONE ROCK HUNTING.

"Bob," Linda gasped, "we waited too long! Those men have run away!"

Hidden Map 5

"We'll notify the sheriff," said Linda. "Maybe Fallon and Hill aren't far away yet!"

"Right," her brother agreed. "But don't you want to find out, if possible, where they headed?"

"I certainly do. Let's inquire next door in the delicatessen," said Linda. "The proprietor may know something about them."

They went into Tony Cocuzza's store. The stout, smiling owner had just placed a roll of spiced meat on a board for slicing.

His round face beamed at the Craigs as he said, "You want to try my fine bologna? It is just ready. Very good."

Linda never felt less like eating—she had just experienced too big a shock from the placard on the gem shop door. She started to shake her head, but Bob gave his sister a warning glance as if to say, We must be friendly to this man!

"That meat looks good and smells great," he said to Tony. "How about making us up a couple of sandwiches to take out?"

"Sì. I make them thick."

Aside Bob said to Linda, "If you don't want yours, I'll eat it."

Linda assured him she would be hungry later. She turned to Mr. Cocuzza. "I see your neighbors at the gem shop have gone on a vacation."

"Those two!" exploded Tony. "What do they need with a vacation? They have only been in the place a few weeks. And they spent a lot of time in here—sitting back there"—he pointed with his knife at the small wooden table in a rear corner—"drinking my coffee and eating prosciutto and cheese."

"I'm surprised to hear that," said Linda. "Mr. Fallon told us he was a sick man—said he had a very bad heart."

Tony gave a little grunt. "Ecco! That fellow never had any heart trouble, and he could eat anything. Ate all the time, he did, and drank lots of coffee. Wanted me to charge everything. Ah! I would not give credit for one pickle to those two. I figured them right away—what you call fly-by-nighters."

"What do you mean?" asked Linda.

"Stay in one place a little while until they get no more credit, then move on suddenly."

"But how could you tell they were like that?" persisted Linda.

Tony looked at her with shrewd black eyes. "They were not businessmen. They had no customers coming in the front door. Men came there, but they went in the back way."

Bob and Linda exchanged looks. "You don't happen to know where Fallon and Hill went, do you?" Bob asked.

"I could not say for sure, but they asked me directions to Granite Mountain," replied Tony. He wrapped the sandwiches. "Here they are. Very good-tasting."

Bob paid him and took the bag. Then he and Linda headed first for the deputy sheriff's office to tell their suspicions, and finally went on to the Highway House to pick up the Old Sol station wagon.

"We sure let Fallon dupe us," Linda said woefully. "The police should have been notified last night."

"Don't feel too bad about it," said Bob. "Fallon and Hill are bound to turn up. I'd say they seem pretty brazen about their work."

"Is Granite Mountain listed in your survey book as a location for mineral gemstones?" asked Linda.

"I think so," Bob replied. "Mr. Hamilton can tell us in a jiffy."

"If it is," said Linda, "I think we should go there rock hunting and see if we can find those thieves. They'll probably hide from the sheriff's men but they might not be so careful about us."

"I'd like to know what they're up to," said Bob. "They may be trying to rob unsuspecting rock hounds out there."

"Even if those two men are the Hamiltons' burglars, they may not have the turquoise and garnets with them. I think they may have sold them."

"That's a possibility," Bob agreed. "If we catch up with them, or the sheriff does, we'll find out."

"Why don't we ask Kathy's father to go along with us?" his sister suggested. "He could show us some rock-hounding tricks."

When they arrived at the Highway House Linda and Bob found Kathy and her father busy in the lapidary shop. Linda told them about the gem shop's being closed and the possibility of Fallon and Hill having gone to Granite Mountain. "Is that a rock-hound location?"

"Yes," said Mr. Hamilton. "It's a favorite, being closer to town and a little easier to reach."

"Bob and I thought we would do some rock hounding out there along with a little sleuthing," said Linda. "We're hoping you'll come along."

"I'd like to very much," said Mr. Hamilton

eagerly. "You know I have a personal interest in wanting to track down those gemstone thieves. The trouble is, I wouldn't be able to leave until day after tomorrow. There's some business here I must attend to."

Kathy spoke up, a smug grin breaking over her face. "Since I'm Dad's secretary I'll have to go along and record the thieves he traps."

The others laughed, and Bob said, "I hope you'll be kept very busy making records."

"In the meantime," said Linda, "we mustn't forget the big midseason gymkhana at the Alpha Ranch to which we've all been invited. It's coming up soon. Our Trail Blazers Club is going to be mighty disappointed if the members don't make a good showing of wins. We'd better do some practicing at Old Sol tomorrow."

Kathy sighed. "I'm just no good at those gymkhana games, so I've decided to enter only the Musical Stalls. But Patches and I will come over and work on that one."

Linda and Bob left for home, each driving a car. Upon their arrival, Doña asked if Fallon and Hill had been apprehended. After hearing the story, she said, "I don't blame you two for feeling chagrined, and I hope you'll redeem yourselves by finding those thieves. But let the sheriff's men take care of the dangerous details."

Later in the day Larry phoned Linda, who brought him up to date on the latest news. She also told of the planned trip to Granite Mountain and the gymkhana practice at Old Sol the following day.

"You'll come?"

"You couldn't keep me away," he declared. "I'll be over early, and I'll also get ready for the Granite Mountain trip."

The next morning the Craigs and their friends assembled at the Old Sol practice ring with Chica, Rocket, Patches, and Gypsy.

"Let's start with Pole Bending," suggested Bob. "That will get us into the swing of the gymkhana." He and Larry went to a shed and brought out six tall poles that had been cemented into gallon cans, and placed them in a row eight feet apart. Linda and the boys cantered in and out among them, around the end, and back, as Kathy recorded the best time.

"It looks as if Bob and Rocket are going to keep the edge on you in this one," she called, giving him a big smile. Then she took Patches on a trot around the poles.

"Why don't you try the bending on a canter?" Bob suggested. "You might be surprised what Patches can do."

Kathy screwed up her face sideways. "And make the worst time of all? No, sir!" she declared. "But seriously, what's the use of practicing for an event I'm not going to enter?"

"Guess you're right," said Linda. "Boys, are you ready for the Keyhole Race?"

Bob took a marker filled with white lime and traced a large keyhole on the ground. This would be another contest against time. The game took a good bit of skill. A rider had to canter through the narrow straight part, pivot in the circle, and canter out again without touching any lime. Chica's dainty hooves helped Linda come out best in this event.

"That was great," said Kathy. "I'm enjoying this show."

Doña had come out to watch, so the riders decided to practice Musical Stalls now. She would start and stop the music on the record player kept in the shed for ring work.

Bob and Larry placed eight-foot two-by-fours on the ground four feet apart to make three stalls. Linda called, "Everyone ready? Get set for the music!"

As soon as Doña started the player, the riders rode around the stalls. When she stopped the record, they raced for the nearest stall.

Of course someone had to be eliminated. This time it was Bob. Rocket was so quick he overshot the stall into which his rider tried to turn him. Linda lost out on the next round, holding Chica back a little so she would not get bumped and marked as a horse usually does. It was for this reason that she did not intend to enter her filly in this event at the Alpha Ranch.

"Come on, Kathy, win!" Linda encouraged her chum, as the contest for the last stall started.

Bob pleaded just as hard with his pal. "Watch your step, old man!"

Kathy had not cantered so fast as the others, but she had developed an uncannily good eye for the empty stall nearest her, and a quick way of turning into it that fooled the rest. When the music stopped she won over Larry in a spurt for the last stall.

"Good work!" cried Linda, and Bob said, "You'll walk off with the trophy at the gymkhana."

"Don't kid me," said Kathy. "Remember, I'll probably be lined up with at least ten hard-riding competitors out there."

"I'm rooting for you," Larry declared.

After a short rest, Linda said, "Let's play the Rescue Race, then call it quits."

For this event the boys would act as "victims" some distance away. The girls would race the horses down the stretch, the boys would leap up behind them, then the animals would run back quickly to the starting line.

Linda rode Gypsy to pick up Larry, and Kathy was astride Rocket to rescue Bob. Rocket was a nose ahead in the race, but slid beyond Bob before Kathy could bring the horse around.

Linda slowed and turned Gypsy just as she reached Larry. He leaped up behind her as she made the turn. The little cow pony was thrown off balance by Larry's sideways landing, made a couple of faltering steps, then lost her balance.

Linda and Larry hit the ground pretty hard on their hips, but rolled free of the horse before she landed full on her side. Gypsy got up immediately and shook herself with no apparent injury.

The others ran to Linda and Larry, asking in unison, "Are you all right?"

The two hastily rose to their feet. "Sure," they replied, but as they walked forward both limped.

"You won't be able to ride to Granite Mountain tomorrow," declared Kathy sympathetically.

Cactus Mac, having seen the accident, came running from the barn. "Sure they can ride," he drawled. "Nothin' wrong with 'em that some good old hoss liniment won't fix."

Larry looked skeptical. "Want to take off my hide, old-timer?" he said, but he was stifling a grin.

Linda laughed. "I'm ready to start soaking in it right now!"

"You go to the house," said Cactus kindly. "I'll help Bob put the horses up."

"I'll run Patches home in the trailer," Bob said to Kathy. "So just unsaddle, and wait until I bring the car back here."

"Thanks," she said with a grateful smile. "That sounds good to me." In a few minutes they set off.

When Bob returned he brought a load with him from the lapidary shop. It included canvas tote bags, small hand mattocks for hacking out unlodged stones, and medium-size paintbrushes to dust dirt from specimens.

"They're for Linda, Larry, and myself," he said. "I hope we get something with these."

"If you don't," spoke up Bronco with a chuckle, "I'll think you're not living up to the Rancho del Sol reputation, and I'm likely to give you extra chores around the place!"

"Guess I'd better not fail." Bob grinned.

Early the next morning the five rock hounds were mounted and ready for the trip. Although Linda and Larry still felt the effects of their spill, riding did not bother them. Bob had led an easygoing ranch horse named Cricket to the Hamiltons' cutoff trail, where Kathy and her father, riding double on Patches, had met him. They went cross-country to shorten the distance to Granite Mountain and arrived there in a couple of hours.

"Where do you suggest we start digging, Mr. Hamilton?" Linda asked. "And don't forget, everybody, we're not only looking for gems, but for Fallon and Hill."

"One place here is as good as another," the lapidary replied.

Kathy spoke up. "The rest of you can look for Fallon and Hill. I'm still going to search for a red-haired man."

"We'd better start some rock hounding so if Fallon and Hill should come along they won't suspect the real reason we're here," said Linda.

Mr. Hamilton picked a spot for digging. "The crystals of quartz are visible," he said. "You might pick out something of value."

They ground-hitched their horses and went to work hacking at the granular rock.

"Follow color as much as you can," Kathy's father directed them.

The young people found mostly ordinary agate or onyx. Kathy finally picked out an unusual-appearing little chunk that her father classified as a bloodstone.

Bob chipped out of the mountainside some small, pretty, round, bluish masses which Mr. Hamilton said were called desert roses.

"They're not used for gems since they're not hard enough to polish," he added.

Linda, who had been working a little distance from the others, called out excitedly, "I think I've found something special!" She moved the specimen back and forth in her hand, fascinated by the play of color from it.

Mr. Hamilton joined her to examine the find. "That's hyalite," he told her. "You probably have a good opal here. That change of color is caused by reflection of the light from the tiny cracks inside the stone."

"I'm lucky!" Linda exclaimed. "Will I qualify as a rock hound?"

"You certainly will, and a good one at that."

At the boys' suggestion, the saddlebag lunches were opened.

"When we finish eating," said Linda, "let's ride around the mountain and look for Fallon and Hill—and 'the red-haired man.' "

Soon after they had started off, the riders came upon a young rock-hound couple who had driven out in a jeep. They said they were Mr. and Mrs. Manos and were hunting for rubies. They had dug out several.

"That's great," said Linda, then asked them, "Have you seen two men out this way—one tall, the other of medium height and build? We thought they might be out here."

"A couple of men answering that description did ride by earlier," said Mr. Manos. "We didn't like their looks. When they asked us what we had found, we told them nothing. We didn't trust them. If they're friends of yours, I'm sorry that we misjudged them."

"They're no friends of ours," said Linda. "We think they're thieves and want to capture them."

"Then I'm glad our rubies were out of sight," said the young woman.

"Did you notice which way they went?" Bob asked.

"They didn't seem too interested in this location," said Mr. Manos, "and mentioned that they were going on to the Shadow Mountains."

"The Shadow Mountains are a long way from here, aren't they?" Linda asked, and Mr. Hamilton nodded. "I guess we can't go there today."

Disappointed, yet delighted to have the clue to the whereabouts of the suspects, Linda and her friends headed for home. As they were riding down a mesquite-fringed wash Bob suddenly stopped, calling out, "Look! Under that bush! A saddle!"

He and Larry dismounted and examined it. The saddle was an old one of worn, roughed-up leather. The cinch was broken, but the tree seemed good.

"I think I'll take this home and re-cover it," said Larry.

"I'll give you a hand," Bob offered.

The riders went directly to Old Sol, where they had been invited to supper. Mrs. Hamilton had also come over to join them there.

Larry took the old saddle out by a corral, near which a ranch hand was burning trash, and dumped it on the ground. After the young people had taken care of the horses, the boys returned to examine the saddle. Bob started to rip off the old covering to check on the wood of the tree. Linda and Kathy stood by watching with interest.

"Paper was used in the padding," Linda remarked. "That's odd."

Larry pulled out one piece of paper, and exclaimed as he looked at it, "This isn't padding. It's a hand-drawn map!"

"Someone hid it in there!" cried Linda.

They all scrutinized the map but did not recognize the spot it indicated.

Linda ran to get Cactus Mac, and Larry handed him the map. "Is this area familiar to you?"

Cactus studied the paper silently for several moments. "Looks like it may be the Shadow Mountains to the nor'east," he said. "And these markin's could be indicatin' some sort o' mineral deposits. I've seen 'em before on maps."

Linda broke in excitedly. "Mr. Hamilton told us that the ancient Indian turquoise deposits were in those mountains! Perhaps these marks on the map show where more of that valuable turquoise is located!"

"You could be right," said Cactus, and returned the map to Larry.

As he spread the crumpled paper out on the ground beside the saddle, a sudden breeze lifted it and sent the map hurtling into the fire!

Flash Flood 6

With lightning quickness, Linda leaped after the map and snatched the paper from the fire just as it settled into the licking flames.

After a hasty look at the map, she said in relief, "It may smell a little smoky, but the paper hasn't even been scorched."

"You sure saved the day," said Larry. "I suppose now you'll claim the secret treasure."

Linda grinned. "I think I'll wait until I see it. At the moment it's still a big mystery."

Just then Mr. Hamilton, who had been walking about the ranch, joined the group.

"Maybe Dad can help solve it," said Kathy.

Linda handed him the map. "We found this hidden under the leather covering of that old saddle. Cactus Mac thinks it may be the Shadow Mountains turquoise deposits."

"I'd say Cactus is probably right," Mr. Hamilton agreed. "And that location is one which will always be of interest to historians, archeologists, and, recently, rock hounds."

"Could you tell us something more about it?" asked Linda.

"Very little is actually known," replied Mr. Hamilton. "But many years before the Mohave tribes of Indians settled in that region, a more cultured ancient people arrived from a southern section of the country. They were related to the Pueblo Indians. It is assumed they were the original discoverers of the turquoise deposits there.

"Many of the turquoise-bearing porphyry veins were under a deep overburden. The ancients were compelled to dig deep pits to the bedrock and break up the hard porphyry with stone picks and mauls. The debris had to be carried out by body slings and in baskets."

"I love the old Indian jewelry I've seen," said Kathy. "Would any of it date back that far?"

"It could. Those people were a very artistic race, as evidenced by artifacts and relics they left behind. The Indians' use of turquoise as ornaments gave them prestige, and it also became highly valuable in trade."

"Anything as difficult to get as that turquoise should have been of high value," said Bob. "How deep did they have to go for it?"

"Some of their larger pits measured twelve feet in depth, and were twenty feet in diameter," Mr. Hamilton explained. "There is always a great deal of interest in the pits. Just the other day a couple of amateur photographers who were in our restaurant for lunch were talking about them. They thought of going there to take pictures. I told them all I knew."

"Oh, Mr. Hamilton, you've given me a terrific idea!" said Linda, her eyes bright with excitement.

"Whoa, gal!" drawled Cactus Mac. "Don't let it throw you."

Linda laughed and said, "If Mr. Hamilton was talking to some people in his restaurant about the turquoise deposits, and if Fallon and Hill were in there eating, they could have overheard it all. So maybe that's why they decided to investigate the area, hoping to find some valuable turquoise that had been overlooked.

"What I would like," Linda went on, "is for Kathy, Larry, Bob, and me to make a trip to Shadow Mountains and try to find these locations indicated on the map. If Fallon and Hill are around there, well—"

"We'll nab them!" Bob finished the sentence.

"Yes, and if they have that Persian turquoise with them, we'll get it back for Charlie Tonka."

"A great idea," agreed Kathy. "But if those men have guns, count me out!"

"I'm with you, Linda, all the way," Larry declared.

"I hope," said Kathy, "that way isn't down a steep twelve-foot pit."

The others laughed. At that moment Luisa came to ring the old musical mealtime bell hanging on the patio wall.

"Suppertime!" Linda called out.

Immediately the riders went to wash up and change their clothes. Then Linda and Kathy helped carry the food out to the patio serving table. Since it was a warm evening, supper would be served outdoors.

Luisa's fine Mexican specialties for this occasion included a big bowl of guacamole dip and crisp quarters of tortillas to eat with it. There were frijoles, enchiladas, tostadas, and a large Mexican skillet casserole of pork, beef, green peppers, and tomatoes. Two big blue pitchers of chilled goats' milk supplied by Luisa's pets Genevieve and Geraldine stood side by side. Those living at Old Sol always drank plenty of this with the highly seasoned Mexican food.

Supper was served buffet style and everyone took a place at the flower-decked patio table. Linda, seated not far from Doña, told her the Shadow Mountains story. "The four of us would like to make a trip there to see those ancient pits, and maybe find some gemstones for ourselves."

Kathy remarked, "Linda certainly has a nice collection started with her garnet and the opal brought back today. Some turquoise would surely be a marvelous addition."

Doña smiled at the girls. "It does sound interesting. But the Shadow Mountains are a considerable distance away, and someone who knows the area should accompany you. Perhaps you can persuade Cactus Mac to go along. If so, the trip has my blessing."

With Cactus along, it has mine too," Bronco replied. His eyes twinkled. "You haven't mentioned that perhaps gemstones aren't the only things you hope to find."

"Oh, it's no secret," said Linda quickly. "We want to locate the thieves who stole the gems from Mr. Hamilton."

Linda was a little fearful that her grandmother might change her mind, but Doña did not seem worried. Mr. and Mrs. Hamilton gave Kathy permission to go, and by telephone Larry's parents consented.

In the meantime, Bob had summoned the ranch foreman and put the question to him. He gave an almost inaudible snicker and said, "Wal now, I could have bet sure money this was goin' to happen when I saw you all huddled around that map."

The young people waited breathlessly to hear his decision.

"Got to go to the stock auction at the Los Angeles stockyards tomorrow," he said. "But I reckon I could make it to get away in a couple o' days to be your trail boss."

"That's wonderful, Cactus. We'll wait," said Linda with a happy smile.

"What will we do with ourselves between now and then?" Kathy asked. "We've exhausted all the clues around Lockwood, there's no word from the sheriff, no horse show—"

The words "horse show" gave Linda an idea. She said to Kathy and Larry, "How about you two staying here overnight and we'll have some real horse fun ourselves tomorrow?"

"A day horsing around," said Larry. "What could be better?"

Bronco laughed. "Is that something different for you four?" he teased.

"I might just think up something different," said Linda challengingly.

"It's plain you've already thought of it," said Larry, "so give."

"How about asking a few of our fellow Trail Blazers Club members to ride over and play broom polo?" Linda suggested.

"Great idea," said Bob. "Some of our neighbors might come to watch. It would be more interesting to have an audience."

"Let's get busy calling right now," Linda answered and hurried inside to the phone.

At one o'clock the next day, two teams were mounted for broom polo practice. One group consisted of the Rancho del Sol four. The other was composed of other Trail Blazers members—Chuck Eller, the president; Sue Mason, the secretary; and Randy and Vicki, two excellent riders. Don Hodder, another member, would referee.

Goalposts had been erected at the two ends of the big corral. Each rider carried a broom to hit the playing ball, a pigskin basketball.

Linda and Sue were chosen captains of their teams and would receive the ball from the referee in the center of the field. The other players were to be spaced about the corral, with one opposing member at each goalpost.

"Bumping another player's horse will count as a fault, and will call for a ten-foot penalty," Don told the players, who nodded.

Each member took a turn at whacking the ball down the field and between the goalposts. It was not easy since the ball often bounced in an unpredictable direction.

Rango sat outside the corral fence watching intently and barking sharply at the ball whenever it angled at a tangent. He growled gutturally and finally stood up with his front paws on the top rail.

When the ball suddenly bounced up and hit him on the nose, he leaped inside the corral and attacked it viciously.

"Outside!" Bob commanded the coyote-shepherd.

Rango scuttled beyond the fence, thumping his tail on the ground in disgruntlement at having been prevented from fighting his enemy.

Patio chairs had been brought to the corral and by two o'clock many of Old Sol's neighbors ringed the fence with Doña, Bronco, and the Hamiltons. A couple of the ranch hands were also present. On a table under the shade of a pepper tree nearby, Luisa had placed jugs of ice-cold lemonade and a large tray of her delicious Mexican molasses cookies.

"Ready, everybody?" called Don to the riders.

"Ready," they answered in unison.

Don placed the ball in the center of the field and blew the whistle. With fleet agility, Linda whisked it with her broom toward the Old Sol goal. It did not get far. Chuck Eller rode in to send the ball back toward the Trail Blazers goal. From then on the ball was brushed back and forth and around the ring at a furious pace.

The first quarter ended without a score. When the half was over it stood three to two in favor of the Trail Blazers. Chuck Eller was a master at the game and had scored all the points. The riders took a twenty-minute break for rest and refreshments.

"This is heaps of fun," said Vicki.

"Yes, and try to beat us," Randy dared Linda's team with a wide grin.

When the whistle blew again the teams changed goals. The Rancho del Sol foursome drove right through to win a point, tying the score. There it held until the last of the fourth quarter. In those moments it appeared as if Old Sol were about to score again.

One well-placed broom smack should send that ball sailing between the posts! thought Linda.

Out of the corner of her eye she spotted Rango, who stood close to the corral. Suddenly he leaped over the fence almost onto the ball, and with his nose started it rolling rapidly up through the clear field to the opposite goal.

"No, Rango, no!" screamed Linda, turning Chica d'Oro after him. "This is our goal down here!"

The dog's intent was not to be defeated this time. In another second his nose had been quicker than goalkeeper Larry's broom, and Rango sent the ball between the posts. Everybody laughed and applauded, and Rango stood with his tongue hanging out, his wide mouth curved in a grin.

"Traitor," said Kathy. "You're supposed to be on our team."

When the laughter subsided, Don asked, "Does

that make the score four to three in favor of the Trail Blazers or do you play the last two seconds over again?"

Chuck Eller replied, "Since a fifth member on a team is illegal we can't count that score. I'm afraid that after this performance we wouldn't get any-place in two seconds. How about calling it quits, and the score a tie?"

"Fair enough," said Bob, and the others agreed.

"Rango," called Luisa, who had been watching. He bounded happily to her. "You are one smart dog," she said and gave him two cookies.

That evening the four young people sat poring over the strange map again. Most of the markings were in wavy circles. Suddenly Linda's gaze picked up a difference in one of them. She pointed.

"This isn't the same shape as the others. It is a broken circle and looks very much like a horse-shoe."

"I'll go along with that," said Larry.

"It must have some special meaning." Linda spoke thoughtfully. "Do you suppose that could be a place where the most valuable mineral rock is located?"

"We'd better make special note of it and try to find that exact spot," Bob declared.

That evening Cactus Mac returned from the cattle auction with the big stock truck full. He unloaded the short-legged, broad-chested animals under floodlights in a small corral. Everyone hurried out to inspect them.

"Fine critters," said Cactus. "No better bunch o' Hereford yearlin's around here."

Bronco inspected them with pleased approval. "Very good buys," he commented.

Presently Linda asked, "All set for the trip tomorrow, Cactus?"

"I sure am an' rarin' to get in the saddle. Trucks are okay but give me a hoss anytime."

The first part of the morning the four young people and the foreman loaded supplies onto three pack horses for their long ride to Shadow Mountains. There was a generous supply of food. Since it was possible the weather might be inclement, Cactus was including a couple of small tents and told the riders to take extra clothing. Bob packed his shortwave two-way radio in one of his saddlebags.

He was wearing old jeans and a T-shirt while helping to load up. Now he went in to change and came back in a bright pink Mexican shirt with a black zigzag design on it that had been sent him as a gift from Mexico. Although it was uncommonly loud, Bob secretly liked the bright color. He said it gave him a lift.

"Wow!" exclaimed Larry, blinking his eyes at it. "Even the stones will groan."

"No danger of losing you," said Kathy.

"Just don't try." Bob grinned.

"Mount up an' ride out," commanded Cactus Mac. "Bob an' Larry, each o' you grab the lead line o' one o' the pack hosses."

Bronco and Doña waved the riders good-bye. "Keep in touch with us," said Tom Mallory.

"With everything in our favor," said Cactus Mac, "we ought to make it to Charlie Tonka's the second night out."

"Nothing makes Charlie happier than to have a bunch ride in," Linda said in fond memory of her stay at the old Indian's cabin.

The riders found the going pleasant until late afternoon. Then the sky turned brassy and the air became humid. Within a few minutes a dark, copper-tinged cloud had obscured the sun. Without the warning of a sprinkle, copious sheets of rain suddenly came down with cloudburst intensity.

"Ride for the cliff!" shouted Cactus Mac. "Follow me!" He went off at a gallop.

In a matter of seconds, the ground was under the raging water of a flash flood. Branches and uprooted small trees surged down from an arroyo to one side of them.

Linda and Chica d'Oro, bringing up the rear, were caught broadside. The debris tangled in the palomino's legs, piling up and trapping her so she could not move. The mud from the channel heaped in mounds about the horse and her rider.

"Help!" Linda cried out as the horror of their situation dawned on her.

But the other riders were far ahead. They did not know of her predicament and might not hear the cry.

In another few minutes she and Chica d'Oro could drown!

Indian Charlie Disappears 7

For a couple of seconds Linda was frozen with terror. How could she escape the torrent that held her and Chica fast?

She urged and coaxed the horse to no avail. The palomino was enmeshed in the snarl of litter matted around them. The filly gave an anguished high scream and Linda started yelling as loudly as she could.

"Bob! Larry! Help!"

The groove in which she and Chica had been caught was quickly becoming a deep trench, cut by the torrent of water from the arroyo channel. Chica's body was covered. Linda, exerting all her might, held the horse's head above water with the reins. She felt her strength ebbing rapidly.

"Help! Help!" she cried amidst the rushing water.

Then she heard Bob's familiar voice call, "Hold tight!" and he came into view.

Larry was beside him. The boys made sure of staying on higher ground and not slipping into the torrent where they would be as helpless as Linda. Their two ropes snaked out, one settling over Chica's neck, the other around Linda.

"Dally them on the saddle horn!" shouted Bob.

Linda quickly did this and the boys backed hard. Finally they hauled the palomino from the ditch. Bob dismounted and removed the tangled mass of mud and branches from between Chica's legs.

"Is she badly cut?" gasped Linda.

"Doesn't look like it," her brother replied. "Just a number of small scratches."

"Oh, good." Linda sighed in relief, then slumped over her saddle, exhausted.

Bob and Larry, riding as close to each side of her as possible, led the way to where Cactus and Kathy, unaware of what had happened, were waiting. The foreman had unloaded the tents and was ready to put them up against the downpour. But as quickly as the deluge had started, it stopped, and a weak sun came out.

Kathy ran to Linda. "Goodness, what happened to you?" she cried in alarm, and helped her friend slide off Chica d'Oro.

"We—nearly—drowned!" Linda replied shakily, leaning against her horse and breathing hard. The filly hung her head low.

Cactus Mac blanched under his tan at the thought of Linda's narrow escape. "Pesky flash floods—thar's nothin' worse for a hoss or a human."

In a few minutes he had one of the tents erected. Cactus tossed in the girls' sleeping bags and their waterproof clothing packs.

"Into dry clothes, both of you," he ordered, "and you, Linda, into the bag."

She did not argue. Larry had already rubbed down Chica d'Oro and covered her with a blanket.

Bob had started a fire. Linda thought she had never felt anything so good in her life as the feel of the dry clothes she put on and the soft, warm sleeping bag into which she slipped. Kathy came in with a cup of hot bouillon she had heated in the tin.

As Linda drank the hot broth, her shivering stopped, and almost immediately she fell asleep. A while later the odor of supper cooking awakened her. She hurried outside and greeted the others with her usual bright smile.

"Hello, everybody! What day is it? I slept so hard I really don't know."

The others laughed. "You've lost only a few hours," said Larry.

Linda noticed that the horses had been tied to a

picket line. She went immediately to Chica, who welcomed her with a soft nicker. The filly was in fair shape. After a rubdown, the palomino's legs had been well powdered with BFI healing powder, and she had been fed.

When Linda returned to the fire, Larry asked, "Will you have your supper in a feed bag or on a plate?"

"I'll take a plate, thanks. I'm allergic to raw oats!" she retorted.

"You win," he said, handing her a generous serving.

The hungry travelers seated themselves on rocks around the blazing fire. Night came on clear and warm with the myriad of stars hanging low.

"We've lost time," said Cactus. "Anyone object to takin' off at dawn?"

"I'm for it," said Linda, and the others agreed.

Later that night, Linda, a light sleeper, was awakened by the restless shuffling of the horses' feet. Then came the quick, disturbed whinnying of Chica d'Oro, which indicated something strange was near.

Quickly Linda jumped up and ran from the tent. The shadowy figure of a man who had been approaching the tents turned and sped away. Linda raced back for her strong flashlight, but by the time she returned and darted the beam about, the figure had vanished. Cactus and the boys were now out with their own lights, but the intruder was not discovered.

"He could be hiding in one of the deep gaps in that cliff," said Bob. "I think it would be useless to try following him tonight."

"Waste o' time," agreed Cactus. "It'd be easy to hide hosses or a jeep back in thar, too."

Linda checked Chica d'Oro, fondling her. "You certainly saved us from some kind of harm, baby. You're a good sentry." The palomino nuzzled her nose in Linda's neck and whinnied softly.

Kathy had not awakened. In the morning when they told her about the nocturnal visitor, she looked alarmed. But upon hearing that no harm had come to the camp, she grinned. "Glad I didn't lose any of my beauty sleep," she said.

Linda had been scrutinizing the hard-packed damp ground. "Here are a man's footprints," she said at last.

The others rushed to her side. The distance between the prints denoted a tall man with a long stride.

"Look!" cried Kathy, pointing to a nearby dead bush on which a few human red hairs were visible. "That red-haired man again! And I didn't catch him!"

Linda gazed at the hairs thoughtfully. "These are so low on the bush they would have been caught only if the man was crawling. That intruder last night was walking. Do you know what I think?"

"What?" asked Larry.

"That these hairs were deliberately left here to fool us about the true identity of the man."

"Just as he did in Dad's shop!" Kathy exclaimed.

Bob tore off a small piece of waxed paper from a sandwich and wrapped the hairs in it. "I'll take this evidence along."

After a quick breakfast, the rock hounds loaded their gear and were soon on their way. Cactus had worked out a shortcut which he declared would take them to Charlie Tonka's quicker than by the regular route.

They arrived early in the afternoon. To their disappointment, Charlie did not come running out to meet them. The visitors sensed an atmosphere of desertion hanging over the place.

"I guess this is Charlie's day to be at the other end of the gas line he inspects," said Linda.

"Probably," said Bob, "but he might be ill."

Linda hastily dismounted. "I'll find out." She ran to the cabin. Charlie's door was never locked, and after knocking, she went in. Linda returned immediately, a look of fright on her face. "Charlie's gone and the cabin is a shambles!"

The others joined her instantly and stared nonplussed at the overturned furniture and small broken objects on the floor.

"Charlie sure put up a fight," said Cactus, "but some critter must'a dragged him away."

"But who—who would do such a thing to Indian Charlie?" asked Kathy.

"We'd better try to find out—and soon," said Linda. "Let's see if we can locate any tracks."

They found many strange horseshoe prints just outside the cabin. They led down the hill.

"We'll follow 'em soon's we've unloaded," said Cactus. "Give a hand, everybody."

Linda and her friends unloaded the packhorses and turned the animals into a corral. Then the riders started off again, following the horseshoe prints. The group separated.

Linda thought she saw the tracks branch off to the right and turned around a butte to investigate. The prints were faint in the silt, but she traced them into a draw.

This would be a good place for an outlaw to hide, she thought, and rode into it.

There were a couple of horseshoe prints, then nothing more. On closer scrutiny, Linda decided that the marks had been made sometime before, and not by the horses they were trying to follow.

She rode out again and stopped. Suddenly Linda was completely confused by the maze of high rocks about her. From which direction had she come?

She called, "Halloo, halloo!" and listened intently for an answer from her companions. But none came.

Linda realized with a slight feeling of panic that she was lost. Now what do I do?, she thought.

She began to recall a list of survival tactics learned years before. The clearest was the advice of Cactus Mac. "When a person's lost he should hunt for a creek and then follow it downstream. The water'll usually lead to a ranch house or settlement or even a road."

Linda had noticed a small stream back in the draw. After vainly calling her friends again, she rode toward it and followed the little stream. It wound through rugged country of boulders and mesquite.

After a while the aroma of cooking reached her. Warily she rode toward two men crouched over a fire preparing their dinner. Two horses were tethered nearby.

Linda wondered whether to turn and retrace her steps, pass the men and go on, or stop to eavesdrop. Just then they looked up in surprise and saw her. Both were middle-aged and kindly-looking.

"You lost?" one asked with a smile.

Linda drew in her breath. She did not want to admit this to the strange men.

"My friends are near," she answered. "I'm just taking a little side trip."

"Light and eat," invited the other man.

"No, thank you," said Linda. "I really have to be riding on."

The first man stood up with his skillet, which was full of fried rabbit. "Huntin' was good today, and I'm good at fixin' it if I do say so myself." He grinned. "Here, try a piece, and tell me whether I'm speakin' the truth or not."

The rabbit had been deliciously browned and smelled tempting. Linda saw that it had been rolled in cornmeal and, from the rashers of bacon piled high on a plate, it had apparently been cooked in bacon drippings.

She rode closer and, leaning from the saddle, took a small piece of rabbit. "Um-m-m, this is wonderful," she said, after chewing the savory morsel.

Linda decided to question the men as to whether or not they knew anything about Indian Charlie.

"My friends and I," she explained, "are trying to locate an old Indian acquaintance of ours who seems to be missing. His name is Charlie Tonka. Have you seen him?"

"Not close up," replied one of the men. "But we did see a couple o' horsemen a while back. They were some distance away. One of 'em was leadin' a horse with its rider strapped in the saddle."

"We figured," said the other man, "that he'd been injured. We tried to catch up with the bunch, thinkin' we might help, but they didn't hear our calls and then we lost 'em."

Linda was convinced that the bound rider was

Charlie Tonka. "Which way were they going?" she asked.

"Toward the north. They were on the trail that crosses the stream a ways down when we lost 'em."

Linda felt sure the pair had seen these men following them and had quickly hidden.

"Thank you very much," she said. "And thanks for the rabbit treat."

Linda rode until she came to the path crossing the stream. Here she stopped, wondering if she should follow it up or down. Which way had Charlie been taken? With no clues to help her, Linda decided to keep on riding downstream.

Suddenly Chica d'Oro pricked up her ears. Linda listened and heard Bob's faraway voice calling her.

"Halloo, halloo," she called back with a great surge of relief, and soon she was reunited with her brother and the others.

"What were you a-followin'—bear tracks?" asked Cactus with a grin.

"Only horses'," she replied. "But they did lead me to what may be some information about Charlie."

She told of her encounter with the rabbit hunters and what they had said.

"It certainly sounds as if those riders they saw had Charlie with them," said Bob.

"But where are they now?" asked Kathy.

Cactus Mac had been scouting around. "Looks

mighty like they went sojournin' off thar in the bushes to hide till nobody was lookin' and then went on up the trail."

"Come on, let's follow them!" Bob urged.

The riders picked up the tracks on the trail, but in a short time the horseshoe prints vanished.

"Those men must've ridden off into the brush again," said Cactus. "Thar'd be no prints to guide us in that ground clutter o' leaves an' twigs. We'd better return to Charlie's cabin an' make a fresh start tomorrow."

Just then a low, uncanny, prolonged sound reached their ears.

Kathy shuddered. "How horrible!" she cried.

The sound came again.

"I've never heard an animal make that kind of a noise," said Larry.

"It certainly is eerie," Linda admitted.

As the weird wail was repeated, the riders sat tense and alert.

A Sidewinder Scare   8

After listening for a full minute, Linda said, "That sound is something like an owl's. What do you think, Cactus?"

The searchers' trail boss had been frowning in deep concentration. After the sound came again, he said, "I'm thinkin' it's not bird or beast or fowl. I believe the sound is bein' made by a human."

"By Charlie's captors?" asked Larry.

"To scare us off?" Kathy suggested.

"It's possible," replied Cactus. "But in olden times Indians used to hoot like owls to call for help."

"You mean," cried Linda, "that the sound could have come from Indian Charlie asking us to help him?"

"And he used the owl sound so his captors wouldn't be alerted," Bob added.

"That's my idea," Cactus replied.

"Let's follow the sound and find him!" Linda urged.

Cactus led the way. "Listen careful, everyone, an' keep your eyes open."

"Nothing like riding into trouble with our eyes wide open," Kathy whispered to Bob.

"Keep behind me and you'll be that much farther from danger," he answered.

"Take it slow and easy," Cactus called back.

The drawn-out dismal cries began to sound closer.

"We're certainly on the right track," murmured Linda.

Whenever a fallen dead branch cracked under a horse's hoof, everyone jumped.

"Uncanny is the word for it," said Kathy with a shudder.

Suddenly Chica d'Oro whinnied and Linda, directly behind Cactus Mac, cried out, "Oh! There he is!"

To the left of the riders stood Charlie Tonka, bound with ropes to a tree. He was drawn-faced, his dark eyes fierce and his black hair disheveled from the struggle he had been through.

Joy came into his face, however, at sight and recognition of the riders. "I heard you coming long way back," he said. "I called to bring you here. I hoped it be good friend."

Linda and Bob had jumped from their horses and

rushed to the Indian. "Charlie! Charlie!" Linda cried. "I'm so glad we found you. Are you all right?"

"I am good now," he responded. The lean, bony Indian looked fondly at Chica d'Oro. "My little palomino pay me back. I saved her mother till she is foal, now Chica help save Charlie."

Bob meanwhile had whipped out his hunting knife and cut the ropes from around Charlie.

"Where are the men who brought you here?" asked Cactus Mac sharply, darting his eyes about.

"They rode off. They not come back now," said Charlie, flexing the muscles of his arms.

"I'm glad," said Kathy in relief.

Charlie went to stroke Chica d'Oro. "Here is my young 'un. And she looks so fine."

"She's a grand show horse now, Charlie," said Linda.

Changing the subject, the Indian asked, "Why are you here?"

"We went to your cabin," Linda explained, "and saw there had been a fight. So we went out to hunt for you."

"That was good," said the Indian. "Thanks."

"What happened, Charlie?" asked Bob. "Who were your attackers, and what did they want from you?"

Charlie shook his head. "Bad men they were— two of them. One was tall and hawk-faced. Other was medium-size and look dumb, but mean. They came to cabin yesterday. Wanted to talk some business with Charlie, they say.

"I think they are good men. I ask them to come in, and I give them coffee. Most time I talk only to my horse, so it is good to have men to talk to.

"Then the tall one say, 'We have seen the valuable green turquoise you took to Hamilton, gemstone dealer.'" The Indian nodded at Kathy. "Your pappy."

Charlie ran his tongue over dry lips. "Man said he would pay me much money to lead them to the place where turquoise was found. I tell them I don't know—it came from my father, and he did not tell me where he get it.

"They not believe me. They say I better remember where my father find turquoise. I say, 'How can I tell you what I do not know?'

"Again they say I lie—that I know where stone come from and they know how to make me talk. They hit me.

"I try to get away—they act like crazy men. I think they beat me till they kill me, and always ask where to find turquoise." Charlie looked down sadly. "But I do not know.

"They knock things over. When I am not looking, one hit me on my head with something hard. Next I know, I am tied up good on my horse, and we ride away someplace."

"The descriptions of those men certainly sound

like Fallon and Hill," said Linda to her friends.

"Did one of them have red hair?" Kathy asked.

"No red hair," Charlie replied. "All brown—dark brown."

"Where did the men take you first?" asked Linda.

"Here in hills. They say they make me prisoner till I show them way to turquoise deposits. I say nothing. I know sometime I could find way to escape.

"Nighttime come. They make camp but give me nothing to eat or drink 'cause I will not talk. They have guns so I do not try to break away.

"In morning they give me no coffee or bread. Still I do not talk. They say guess I do not know anything to tell them. But they do not want me to go free. Might set someone on their trail.

"They tie me up to that tree and turn my horse Jim loose. Then they tell me not to call for help till evening. They have partner hiding to guard me and he will shoot."

Charlie smiled. "I do not think so, but take no chance. I do not call like human—bad men might hear and come back. I make call like hoot owl. I think desert people know big hoot owl not found here—only little desert owl. Somebody hear and come to find me. You are good friends to Charlie. We have not seen each other in long time. We go back now to cabin and make big feast."

Charlie started to walk off but swayed from

faintness. Linda brought him water from the canteen in her saddlebag, then a handful of nourishing peanut cookies.

"I will be all right now," the Indian insisted.

"Here, Charlie," commanded Bob, "you ride in Rocket's saddle, and I'll sit behind."

Charlie gave him a grateful nod and climbed up. When they reached the cabin, the girls righted the overturned furniture while the men took care of the horses. Linda hastily made coffee, poached eggs, and toast to bolster Charlie until they could get dinner ready.

"You spoiled Charlie with good cooking last time you were here," he said. "Now you do the same again. Thanks."

Linda looked out the window and saw Jim, Charlie's black Tennessee walker, slowly ambling up the hill.

"Here comes your horse, Charlie!" she cried happily. "He found his way home."

"Good," he said, and he followed Linda outside.

Jim's eyes were dull and his head hung low. Apparently he was dispirited at being turned away from his master and from the task of finding his own way home.

"Come, Jim," said Charlie, "you will get hay and corn."

Jim did not respond with his usual show of

affection for Charlie. He seemed to be suffering a mistrust of all humans.

"I think I know what will cheer him up," said Linda. She brought back Chica d'Oro from the small corral back of the barn and put her in Jim's paddock.

Instantly his head jerked up and sparkle returned to his eyes at the sight of his former stablemate. Chica whinnied with unrestrained gladness as she danced to him. They rubbed their heads over each other's necks. Jim had become his old self again!

Bob thought Charlie's capture should be reported, so he got out his shortwave two-way radio and called Rancho del Sol. Doña answered and said she would talk to Deputy Sheriff Wilkins at Ruddville, the nearest town to Charlie's cabin. Mrs. Mallory then reported news from the New York police that Fallon and Hill were wanted there for passing bad checks.

"One more reason for nabbing them," said Bob. "How's everything at home?"

"Everything's going well here at the ranch," she assured Bob before signing off.

Charlie had a fine big chunk of corned beef curing in a little wooden tub of brine, and several heads of cabbage were on hand. He insisted they use them for dinner. With baked potatoes and stewed prunes for dessert, it was a feast.

Everyone went to bed early. The men slept in the

main room of the cabin, while the girls put their sleeping bags on two of Charlie's folding cots in his storeroom.

In the morning, Linda got out the map and showed it to Charlie. "Does this look familiar to you?" she asked. "Cactus and Kathy's father believe it represents part of the Shadow Mountains area."

"This is so," confirmed Charlie. "I went there with my father when little boy. I see those pits that were dug long time ago. No turquoise there then. All worked out by tribes long time ago."

"But what about this different marking?" asked Linda. "A circle with the small section of line out of it. Would you know what that might mean?"

"Yes, I know," said Charlie. "That is sign the work not finished. Maybe it means all turquoise not taken out of pit."

"How thrilling!" cried Kathy. "Why, that means we might obtain some valuable turquoise if we can locate this spot!"

"Fallon and Hill may know about the place also," said Bob.

"Ah, those bad men!" exclaimed Charlie. "They talk all time. Say they go to Shadow Mountains."

"Let's hurry and find that unworked pit before they do!" Linda pleaded.

"You will not stay with Charlie longer?" the Indian asked dolefully.

"We better get goin' after them varmints," declared Cactus Mac.

Linda smiled warmly at Indian Charlie. "We'll come back soon."

There was a long stretch of desert to cross before the riders turned into hill country again. Everyone rode relaxed, not talking much. It was so still that the faint crunch of the horses' hooves in the sand sounded loud.

Suddenly, close to Patches, a small, tan snake, a sidewinder, went scooting out of the path rattling its nether end angrily. Patches shied five feet, and in her panic grabbed the bit in her mouth. She took off over the desert like a racehorse.

"Oh!" cried Linda. She could see Kathy trying to bring the horse around, but to no avail.

Instantly Bob dropped his packhorse line and spurred his own mount after Kathy.

Linda was frowning worriedly. "Oh dear, I hope she can ride it out."

"Kathy will," said Cactus, "if she sticks with her hoss."

"Bob is gaining a little to the side of her now," said Larry. "He'll cut in and stop that little paint in a few seconds."

Bob did just that, grabbing a firm hold on Patches' bridle. "Hey," he said to Kathy with a laugh, "don't you like the company you've been traveling with?" Then he sobered. Kathy's eyes were enormous, and she was white as alabaster. "Are you all right?" he asked solicitously.

"I will be when my heart stops pounding," she gasped.

Soon her fright was gone and Bob turned to his usual teasing. "You've had good practice for one of those 'race for time' gymkhana trophies," he said.

Kathy gave him a look under lowered lids. "From here out I'm hitching on to the packhorse string," she declared.

Bob kept a firm hold on Patches as he turned her around, but saw there was no danger of her spurting off. She was heaving from the run, and was very docile. By the time Kathy and Bob returned to the others, the warm apricot glow had come back to her face. After a short rest the rock hounds started off again.

They stopped for a cold lunch and staked up a tarp for some shade. Cactus Mac checked the state survey map put out for desert travelers, to find the location of the nearest campsite where they might spend the night.

It was late afternoon when they rode into the spot. Water was bubbling up from a mass of rocks, coursing a distance through rabbit brush, and disappearing into the sand again.

After supper Linda said, "I wonder where Fallon and Hill are tonight. It worries me that they may already have dug out the turquoise deposit and vanished."

"Worry 'bout things like that," said Cactus Mac, "is what keeps folks awake at night. Yup. That's the way 'tis. You just better be puttin' such ideas out'n your mind till sunup."

Linda took the trail boss's advice and slept soundly until suddenly something fell heavily on her. It covered the two girls completely.

Springing awake, Linda cried out in a muffled voice, "The tent! It's down! Kathy! Where are you?"

As Kathy gurgled a reply, Linda pulled herself from under the canvas. She was immediately knocked over by a terrific rush of hot wind blowing with tornado force.

The camp had been turned into a shambles. Both tents had whipped down on their occupants. The spooked horses were whinnying in fright and trying to break loose from their picket line!

A Thrilling Discovery   9

As quickly as Cactus, Bob, and Larry could move, they scrambled out from under their canvas. Bracing themselves against the terrific hot wind, they dashed to pull the other fallen tent from Kathy and helped the frightened girl to her feet.

By this time Linda had risen, keeping her back to the wind. She and Kathy stood on top of the tents until the others could anchor the canvases with rocks to keep them from being blown across the desert.

"Duck, everybody!" Linda cried out suddenly.

She spotted a swirling dust devil being raised by the furious wind and coming their way. In the pale light of dawn, the distant mountains vanished in the dust-laden air, and the heaving sand looked like an angry sea.

The conical mass skirted the camp by a few feet.

When it was gone, the four young people scurried to retrieve their possessions and put them in one pile. The boys dragged a tent over the heap and firmly weighted it down on all sides with rocks. Then blankets were quickly thrown over the horses to afford them some degree of protection.

"Goodness, where do such winds come from so suddenly?" gasped Linda. "It's as hot as heat coming right out of a furnace!"

"That's a good question," said Kathy. "I don't think it comes from anyplace—just seems to happen. But it usually whips up only in the spring or fall, not summertime."

Cactus Mac, who had come over to check on the packs, said, "Kathy's part right. This is a desert wind for sure, but it's comin' from the east, an' is called a santana. That's the Indian name an' means the big hot blow. Folks today call it a Santa Ana."

"Whatever it is, it's horrible," Linda declared, looking around her as the campers huddled over their pack pile, ducking their heads from the sand-filled air.

Small creosote bushes and pale desert holly were being torn from the desert floor, and swirled along in a melee of debris. Cottontails, little kit foxes, and ground squirrels scurried for what protecting shelter they could find.

Suddenly a prickly honey mesquite was hurled

against Chica d'Oro. She screamed, reared, and broke her halter. In a panic of terror, the filly started to run.

Linda jumped up, crying out, "Chica, stop! Stop!" and dashed after the palomino, the force of the wind helping to speed the girl along.

Chica paid no attention to Linda. Blinded by the sand, the horse galloped aimlessly. In a moment she stepped into a mound of rocks. As a forefoot became wedged between two stones, the filly pulled back on it, whinnying wildly.

Linda reached her in another instant. "Stand, baby! Stand!" she commanded, holding Chica's head close to her own and stroking the horse's pulsating neck to calm her.

The girl's presence, voice, and touch quieted the palomino. The quivering ceased and the terror went out of the filly's eyes. She nuzzled her velvety nose into Linda's shoulder and nickered softly.

When the palomino tried again to pull out her foot, Linda commanded, "Stand!" She thought, If Chica d'Oro should break a single blood vessel in her hoof, it would take months to cure and she couldn't be ridden for a long time!

By now Linda's companions had run up, and Cactus Mac said, "If we can yank one o' these here big rocks loose at the side o' Chica's foot, I reckon she'll be able to pull free."

With Bob and Larry helping, he tugged hard on

one rock in an attempt to work the large stone loose. But it was deeply embedded. They tried other rocks, but they too would not budge. Chica gave a plaintive whinny from time to time.

"Just stand, baby," Linda entreated. "You'll be all right in a few minutes."

Finally Cactus and the boys worked one rock loose. The palomino stepped free.

"Thank goodness!" said Linda.

Kathy had been standing nearby, alternately watching the rescue and gazing around. Now she exclaimed, "Will you look here and read this!"

They turned to see what she had found. An old wooden grave marker, silvery with age, was firmly ensconced in some rocks. Carved into it were the words:

PETE BURKE
Died Aug. 11,1901
Victim of the Elements

Kathy clasped her head in her hands, bracing herself against the santana. "If this wind doesn't let up, we may have the same kind of fate as poor Pete."

"Not us, Kathy," said Bob. "We have equipment to weather this, and know-how to tell us the way to use it. Anyway, the wind's dying down."

Cactus Mac said, "Many o' the old prospectors

sure were greenhorns. They come out in this here desert without proper pertection an' no idea o' the nature o' the place they were comin' to. They figgered food an' water were enough. But they sure weren't. If one o' these here hot windstorms blew their way a poor hombre sometimes just had to gasp it out, not knowin' what to do or which way to turn. This Burke was likely one of 'em. Prob'ly had a pardner who buried him. An' what happened to the pardner—who knows?"

There was a moment of reverent silence, then the rock hounds slowly moved back to the tents.

"Old Santa Ana blows out," said Cactus Mac. "After breakfast we'll pack up an' leave." Holding Chica's mane, Linda led her back to the picket line and Bob fixed the broken bridle with a length of leather thong.

"What's for breakfast?" asked Larry. "That hot wind has given me an appetite."

"Cookin' is out o' the question." said Mac.

Linda was down on her knees, peering under the tent that covered their rescued possessions and feeling around among them. At last she brought out a box of fig-filled crackers. "Breakfast, everyone! Take a handful!"

"Slim pickin's, but they're good," declared Larry.

After eating several of the crackers and drinking tomato juice, the boys hand-fed the horses.

Kathy roamed about restlessly, her eyes on the

desert floor. Bob wondered what she was looking for.

"Think you can find even a crumb on this cleanswept table?" he asked her.

"Want me to show you?"

"If you make it a valuable crumb."

Linda and Larry joined the others, curious to watch Kathy. She became serious in her search.

The ground at this spot was the usual pebble-paved desert floor, its surface composed of dark-colored, smooth-faced pebbles interspersed with tightly packed grains of sand.

Kathy plucked out a small pebble and held it up, saying "Dark outside, bluish-gray inside." She picked up a couple more, slightly different in color inside, but with the same dark color outside.

"All right, professor," said Bob. "Why are they all the same color on the outside?"

She smiled at him knowingly. "The little rain-drops and sunbeams working together have given the surface a thin coating of what is called desert varnish. It is iron-manganese oxide."

"Wow! You really know your stuff!" said Larry.

"You're wonderful to have studied all those fascinating things," said Linda.

"If I had had to study them," said Kathy with a laugh, "they probably would have gone in one ear and out the other. Actually, I grew up learning about rocks by playing with my dad."

Linda and Bob glanced at each other. They too had enjoyed playing with their father, not only in the United States but in various foreign countries, and learning many interesting facts from him. How they missed both him and their mother!

Presently Larry said, "Look how white the sand is that was beneath the pebbles Kathy picked up, compared to the dark gray of the topsoil."

"Watch!" Kathy said.

She bent down and took a few moments to survey the ground. Then she commenced walking about, picking up pebbles and tossing them away to make a design. Presently she stood up with a triumphant nod. Outlined in the white sand was a figure of a cat.

"Fabulous!" exclaimed Linda.

"The prehistoric Indians used to make pictures like this as large as one hundred feet square," said Kathy.

"That must have been something for the birds to see," commented Larry.

"It's too bad there were no airplanes then so a lot of people could have looked at the pictures," said Bob.

"That thar's right nice," declared Cactus Mac. Then, turning his face into the wind, he added, "The santana's about gone."

"It is cooler," Bob remarked.

"Do you think it would be all right to build a small fire now, Cactus Mac?" asked Linda.

"I reckon," their trail boss replied.

The boys erected what they figured was a stout shield against the remaining wind, using the tent stakes and the tarp. Then they scooped out a hole in the sand and built a fire.

"I think this is the time to have the special treat Luisa made for us," said Linda. "It will take only a jiffy to heat."

She brought out the three jars of tasty-looking chicken stew and dumped the contents into a pan. Cactus and the boys hovered hungrily over the savory meal.

Kathy had plates ready. As she handed one to each camper, the wind, as if peeved at not having been able to bring destruction to this intrepid group of humans, suddenly whipped up a new blast. It tore away the tarp shield and filled the pan of chicken stew with sand and dirt!

"Oh, no!" groaned Bob, as Linda failed to keep the pan from overturning.

Everyone looked at the ruined lunch with stunned faces. Then Kathy giggled. "This is what they say builds character!"

"Right now I'm going to build some sandwiches," declared Linda.

She managed to get a stack of them filled with

canned meat. The campers felt better with their hunger relieved despite the last-minute change of menu.

The wind finally died down. By midafternoon, Cactus said it would be all right to proceed on their trek to the Shadow Mountains. The whole group hurried to load up and soon the detective–rock hounds were on their way.

They passed through a section of Joshua trees. Big clusters of pods left from lilylike blooms sprang from the rosettes of sharp-pointed leaves.

When they reached a foothill, Cactus called a halt. "We'll be campin' here," he said. "It's the last water we'll find for a good distance. It's called Scarlet Creek."

"This is one of the most beautiful spots we've seen," said Linda enthusiastically. "It just doesn't seem like a place where gem thieves should be hiding out."

The little creek that rippled along was bordered by reddish cliffs overhung with tall mesquites. There were cacti on the cliffs, with stately pines farther up. Junipers grew on the desert cove side.

Kathy remarked, "It seems as if Nature had a hard time deciding where the desert was to stop and the mountains to begin!"

The others laughed but agreed. As they made

camp, Linda asked, "Why was this named Scarlet Creek? It looks greenish to me."

Cactus glanced at the sky. "In a few minutes you'll be seein' for yourself."

It was not long before the setting sun turned the color of the cliffs a deeper, more vivid red, and the creek brilliantly reflected the same red hue.

"I'm going to paint a picture of this spot as soon as I get home," Linda declared.

It was so pleasant and restful that everyone slept well. They left early the next morning, hopeful that the turquoise mystery would be solved before nightfall. It was an enjoyable journey through interesting colored-rock formations and sprawling green tamarisks.

By late afternoon the riders had reached the foothills of the Shadow Mountains, and pulled in close to one of the peaks. High above them was a towering cliff pockmarked with caves.

Next to the chosen camp spot water spouted from the rocks. Cactus Mac remarked, "This here little geyser's just like most o' the desert streams. See how it disappears underground? It's lookin' for a way to get to the Colorado River."

Kathy giggled. "I don't care where it goes. I'm just glad it comes."

She scooped up handfuls of the water and declared it delicious. After supper, she said, "I think I'll try out Dad's ultraviolet light I brought along. Does anyone want to go up among the rocks with me and see if we can find some that will fluoresce?"

Linda, Bob, and Larry enthusiastically said they did. Cactus Mac shook his head. "Not me. I'm stretchin' out right where I am. I'll look at the purties in the sky."

As the young people climbed, Larry said, "We're always hearing about the violet rays of the sun. Why do many of these mineral rocks fluoresce in bright colors under an untraviolet light and look drab under sunlight?"

Kathy laughed. "The sun is our natural source of violet rays. Dad says that due to the variable conditions of the atmosphere through which the rays must pass, by the time they reach us there's not sufficient intensity left to be useful for observing fluorescence."

"I guess the discovery of this ultraviolet light has helped a lot in the prospecting of valuable metals," said Larry.

"Well-l, not too much," Kathy replied, "because fluorescence is not a positive means of identification for any mineral except tungsten. Whew! I'm glad that lecture is over!"

"You amaze me," said Larry, wagging his head.

With the aid of their flashlights, the searchers climbed up among the rocks.

"Stop here, and turn off your flashes," Kathy directed. She snapped on her ultraviolet light and picked up a brilliant green rock. "I think this is torbernite," she said.

Kathy passed the light to Linda, who tried her luck in several pockets. Presently she detected a beautiful specimen of fiery red, lined with yellow and set in purple.

"Oh, that's gorgeous!" Kathy exclaimed. "It's manganese geode and pretty rare. You'd better take that piece home with you."

Each of the boys took a turn with the light. They picked up the red and green of calcite and willemite, and even some blue azurite.

"This is magic!" exclaimed Larry.

"Like the air," Bob said. "That's full of distant sights and sounds, but it takes radio and television to reveal them to us."

Suddenly Linda gave a cry of alarm. The other three turned quickly.

To their amazement, Linda had disappeared completely!

The Ancient Pit 10

"Linda!" cried Kathy. "Linda! Where are you?"

The boys, puzzled and worried, beamed their flashlights about. Bob was fearful his sister had dropped through an opening in the mountainside.

"Look twice before you move," he cautioned the others, trying to keep his voice calm. "We might be near an excavation."

Kathy and the boys kept calling Linda's name. Finally they heard a faint response.

"Help! Down here. Help!"

The searchers took careful steps in the direction of the voice and came to a small, deep pit. Bob beamed his flashlight below. Linda stood there!

"Are you all right?" he called to her.

Linda looked up, relieved. "I'm all in one piece, but the sides of this pit are too steep and shaly for me to climb out. I take one step up and fall back two."

"We should always carry a rope along when we go into rock hound country," Larry berated himself.

"We'll have to try something else," said Bob. He sat on the edge of the pit, and then dropped down.

Kathy knelt on the rim and called, "Do you see anything of value?"

"That depends on what value you place on Bob and me!" Linda retorted.

Larry laughed. He lay on his stomach peering down. "What can I do to help?"

"I'll hoist Linda to my shoulders," Bob answered. "You grab her hands and pull while she climbs out."

Linda stood on her brother's shoulders and raised her hands, while Larry positioned himself into a firm crouch.

"Get in back of me, Kathy," he said. "Hang on tight around my waist and pull back as Linda starts up."

Kathy did as directed, tightly clasping her hands together about him. Larry took a good grasp of Linda's hands. "Ready! Start climbing!"

Linda dug her toes into the silty side. She slipped and slid but Larry held on and Kathy pulled backward with all her strength. At last Linda stepped over the edge. She and Larry and Kathy tumbled over in a heap.

As they untangled, Larry asked solicitously, "Are you sure you're all right, Linda?"

"Yes, really."

Bob's muffled voice came from the bottom of the pit. "Yoo hoo! Remember me?"

Larry hung over the edge. "We'll remember you to the folks back home if you don't come up with a bright idea on how we're going to get you out of there."

"Roll your jackets tightly, knot them together, and hang the string of them over the rim."

"Okay, we'll try it."

When the jacket rope was ready, Larry said, "Hold on to me, Linda. Kathy, you hang on to her."

Larry dropped down the makeshift line and called, "Okay, Bob, start coming up."

Larry, Linda, and Kathy pulled with all their strength and kept backing, as Bob braced his feet against the side of the treacherous pit and began the ascent. Finally he reached the top.

"Good work. Thanks, everybody."

Linda untied the jackets and found that no damage had been done to them by the tugging.

"They're made for rugged prospectors like us," said Larry.

The four rock hounds went back to where they had been looking at the minerals. Kathy picked up the ultraviolet lamp, which had been dropped in the excitement.

Linda pried out her specimen of manganese geode. "Here, Larry, this is for your rock collection," she said.

"Oh, wait, I can't let you give me that," he protested. "It's too rare."

"Your reward for rescuing me," she said, chuckling. "Anyway, I'm going to keep only gemstones, and since you're collecting rocks, you take it."

"All right then, and thanks."

Kathy sighed. "Linda's collecting gemstones, Larry's collecting rock specimens, I'm collecting bruises, and what are you collecting, Bob?"

"I'm trying for a couple of crooks," he replied.

The foursome discussed Fallon and Hill at length. "They're certainly elusive," Linda declared.

"Don't forget," Bob spoke up, "that this is a big desert."

When he and the others arrived in camp, they found Cactus Mac asleep inside his bag. Apparently he had long since closed his eyes on the "purties" in the sky.

The horses stood dozing quietly, but Linda slipped over to them. She laid her cheek against the side of the palomino's head for a moment and whispered a good-night in her ear. Without moving, Chica d'Oro responded by giving a soft nicker.

In the morning, Cactus again studied the map carefully to determine which way the group should go to locate the spot indicated by the odd horseshoe mark.

"What do you think, Cactus?" asked Linda.

"I can guess at the startin' trail but that's about

all," he replied. "We'll just have t' take a chance an' see what we'll run into thar in backcountry."

In the "backcountry" they went up and down small canyon sides, and from bright sunlight into deep shadows.

"It's plain to see how the Shadow Mountains got their name," said Linda.

"I feel as if I'm on a roller-coaster ride going up and down these hills," Kathy remarked.

The precipices towering above them were so beautiful that no one minded the rugged trail, and the group stopped now and then to admire the magnificent coloring.

"Oh," cried Linda, "would I love to have all these colors on my palette. I've never seen such an array in one place—turquoise, amber, coral—" Suddenly she interrupted herself. "Look, everybody! I see two riders over there to our right."

Bob snapped his eyes from the colorful scene to the horsemen. "Fallon and Hill?"

"Maybe one is the red-haired man," said Kathy.

"It's hard to tell from here who they are," said Linda. "Let's keep riding toward them."

"If they're Fallon and Hill," her brother said, his jaw set, "we'll surround those thieves and search them! If they're not, maybe the two horsemen can give us some information about the ones we're looking for."

A little farther on, Larry said, "I'm sure those

riders aren't Fallon and Hill. Neither of them is tall."

As the rock hounds came near the men, Kathy announced, "I know those riders. They're friends of Dad's—Mr. Warner and Mr. Becker."

The men had waited for the Rancho del Sol group to reach them and were surprised and pleased to see Kathy. She introduced them to her friends.

Then she asked, "Have you seen a red-haired man riding around here?"

"No," replied Mr. Becker.

Linda spoke up. "Did you happen to see two men riding together—one tall with dark hair and sort of a beaklike nose, the other medium height?"

"Neither of them," replied Mr. Becker. "The only men we've seen since we've been riding here are a couple of Indians picking up any salable stuff they could find for their shop on the highway."

"Are you familiar with the distant mountain areas?" Linda asked the men.

"Not much of it beyond this region," replied Mr. Warner. "We're here to pick up a variety of mineral rock that is mostly found in this vicinity. It's for a geological survey. Are you trying to locate some special area?"

"Yes, the spot indicated by an oddly marked place on this map," she replied, extending the paper to him and explaining where they had found it.

Both men studied the map and shook their heads.

"This doesn't mean a thing to me," said Mr. Warner. "I'll make a note of it, though, and if we should happen to run across such a shaped area, we'll drop by your camp and let you know."

"Is there something in that area which your dad is interested in, Kathy?" asked Mr. Becker.

"We don't know what's there," Kathy replied. "We're trying to track it down just for the fun of it."

"Well, good luck," said Mr. Becker, then he and Mr. Warner rode off.

"What do you think now, Cactus?" asked Linda.

"Wal, that thar horseshoe spot could be anyplace 'round here or a long way off," he drawled. "Why don't you young folks just poke 'round here for a while, an' see what you can find? The hosses could do with a rest an' a drink. Thar's a trickle o' water over yonder comin' out o' that crack in the cliff."

"It's about time for our sandwiches too," said Linda. "I see a nice, shady spot under that over-hanging rock. Let's eat and then see what we can find out about this place. It might even contain the turquoise mine!"

After they had taken care of the horses and eaten their ham and egg sandwiches, the foursome started grubbing with their small hand mattocks. Hopeful, they had slung canvas tote bags over their shoulders.

Larry called out presently and everyone hurried

to his side. "I've found something here I think may be a treasure!"

It appeared to be a tool of gray stone completely embedded in another darker rock.

"Doesn't this look like a pick?" he asked.

"Looks like one because it is one," Kathy told him excitedly. "Those ancient Indians who discovered turquoises in these mountains used stone picks of this kind. It's a real relic."

"Turquoise!" exclaimed Linda. "Maybe we've found the spot mentioned on the map!"

Everyone went to work with renewed excitement. Larry, using his mattock and hammer, extricated his souvenir. Not far from him, Linda dug out a couple of odd-appearing stones. They looked as if a round rock had been split in two and the ends of each piece ground sharp. Both were flat inside, and the curved outside fitted into the palms of her hands.

"What do you suppose these are?" she asked.

Cactus Mac had the answer. "Wal, what do you know! You did make a find, Linda. Those stones are a couple o' primitive fist axes. The Injuns held 'em in their hands to chop with. An' they did a lot o' work with 'em too, I'll wager."

In a little while Cactus picked up a colorful shiny object and smiled broadly. "Here's an arrowhead."

Kathy scrutinized the greenish-brown object.

"It's made of petrified wood. Most of the early Indians around here used this to make their arrowheads. It was plentiful, hard, and slick—and deadly when it hit."

"I got no place for clutter in my quarters," said Cactus. "You want it?" he asked Kathy, handing it to her.

"Oh, yes. Thanks," she replied.

"I'll bet your father would love to hang that on the wall of his shop," said Linda.

"He'll get it for Christmas!" Kathy added with a grin.

"There must have been an Indian lodge on this very spot," said Linda. "Let's keep poking about, and see what else we can find. It may lead us to the turquoise treasure."

She was working near the cliff and presently noticed the mouth of a cave almost hidden by the thorny brush. Linda hacked away enough of the brush to step inside and turned on the flashlight she had clipped to her belt. At first there appeared to be nothing of interest in the cave. The damp walls were bare rock.

Suddenly, noticing a crevice in the center of the cave, Linda walked to it and beamed her light up the narrow passageway. As the bright beam traveled over the ceiling, jagged objects caught her eye.

"Arrows!" Linda thought. "How weird!" Excitedly she called out to her friends. "Come quickly! I've found something!"

The others ran into the cave. After they had peered up the long, narrow cleft, everyone concurred that the objects were indeed arrows.

"Thar's plenty of ancient arrowheads found all the time," said Cactus Mac, "but never any shafts. If these here could be got out they'd be worth a fortune."

"I can't understand if they're so valuable why they've been left here," pondered Linda. "Surely prospectors or rock hounds must have discovered them before now."

"The Injuns have a way 'o pertectin' their sacred relics," said Cactus.

"You mean you believe the ghosts of the ancient Indians are still protecting these arrows from being taken away?" asked Linda incredulously.

"That's the legend," said Cactus wryly. "It goes this-a-way—the early Injuns allowed their young men t' take one arrow from the quiver an' shoot it into a crevice in a cave. If it stayed, this here was a sign that the youth had got to manhood, an' he'd be a great hunter. 'Twas said that the Injun ancestors what guard the cave will be hurlin' big rocks on anybody that disturbs the arrows."

Bob grinned. "I think I'll take a chance, and try to get down one or more of these arrows."

"I'd sure like one for my collection," said Larry. "What's your idea on how to reach them?"

"Let's make a long pole and try to poke them loose," Bob suggested.

He and Larry went outside and cut several strong, straight brush limbs. They bound the ends together with long, dry grasses.

Back inside the cave once more, Bob told Linda, "Shine your light up the crevice now."

He poked the end of the pole about among the arrows. "I think I'm getting one!" he exclaimed.

Suddenly his hand slipped and the pole whanged against one of the loosely embedded rocks on the side. It came crashing down, showering dust over the watchers and knocking the light from Linda's hand.

"Get out o' here afore we bring the whole mountain down on top of us!" shouted Cactus. "The Injun spirits are workin'!"

Linda snatched up her light and ran out after the others. "Well," she exclaimed breathlessly, "I guess those arrows are going to stay where they are!"

"What did I tell you?" said Cactus with a chuckle.

The trail boss concluded everyone had had enough rock hounding for the day, so they returned to camp.

Immediately Linda cried, "Someone has ransacked the place!"

Everyone dismounted hastily and stared at the disorder.

Linda at once investigated the provision packs. "The prowler wasn't an animal. All the food is here."

Larry anxiously examined his knapsack. "The intruder wasn't a rock hound. My piece of manganese geode is still here, too."

Cactus Mac had made a hasty check on everything else. "Nothin's gone. Looks to me as if someone was here searchin' for some particular thing. What was it?"

"Probably this map!" said Linda, taking it from her pocket. "And I'll bet our visitors were Fallon and Hill! Do you realize what this means? We've caught up to them!"

"Or they've caught up with us," Larry corrected.

"But how would they have known of the map?" asked Kathy.

There was silence for several seconds, then Bob ventured a guess. "Somehow they heard of its existence and figured the reason we're here is that we're following the directions on it."

"If they try to take this map tonight, they'll have to take me along!" Linda declared. "I'm sleeping with it!"

Later, she put the map into her sleeping bag and dozed off feeling it was safe. Hours later she was awakened by Chica d'Oro whinnying at her from the entrance of the little tent.

"Baby," Linda called softly, "how did you get loose again?" She could see by the moonlight that the bridle was intact.

Linda jumped up and ran outside. At once her attention was drawn to a scene a short distance away. A tall, thin man was standing by a tree, searching the pockets of Bob's jacket, which hung on a low limb!

The Leather Case Clue
11

"What are you doing here?" Linda called out sharply as she moved toward the intruder.

The tall, slender figure straightened up suddenly at the sound of her voice, dropped the jacket, and ran. He jumped into the saddle of a horse standing behind him in the shadows and galloped off.

Cactus Mac, Bob, and Larry came running from their tent. "What's up?" Bob asked.

Linda explained.

"Did you see who the hombre was?" barked Cactus.

"I couldn't see his face in the dark," Linda replied. "But he was tall and thin. That man was searching through your jacket, Bob. I'm suspicious he was Fallon."

Her brother picked up his jacket. "Fallon, eh?

Well, he was disappointed. Most of my pockets are full of dirt." He shook the coat out. "Serves him right."

"What was he looking for?" Larry asked. "The map?"

"Probably," Linda answered.

The conversation brought Kathy from her tent. "Having a party without me?" she asked sleepily.

"We had an intruder," Linda answered, and quickly told what had happened.

"Why is Chica loose?" Kathy asked, going over to the palomino, who was dragging her tie rope.

"I don't know," Linda said, picking up the filly's rope. "That man must have untied her, but I don't know whether he meant to steal my horse or just turn her loose so I would be unable to go very far. In that way I couldn't do any more gem hunting. I think she must have pulled away from him. You know she doesn't like strangers." Linda stroked the golden filly's forehead.

"That fellow didn't have much hoss savvy," said Cactus, "or he would'a known that if he turned only one hoss loose it wouldn't leave the bunch."

Linda fastened Chica d'Oro back on the picket line and then said, "I'm so wide awake now I think I'll sit out here awhile." She stirred the red coals of the campfire with a stick.

"You've got company," said Larry, tossing on more kindling.

Cactus picked up his coffeepot and checked on its contents. "Might as well have a cup before I sack out," he said, setting the pot on the fire.

"I'm wide awake too," declared Bob, dropping to the ground. "Care to join us, Bright Eyes?" he said to Kathy, who was stifling a yawn.

Kathy smiled and sat down. There was silence for a few minutes as the five friends stared into the fire, hypnotized by the flickering red and yellow flames. Then Linda said, "How about spinning us a yarn, Larry?"

"That'll make us sleepy if nothing else does," Bob remarked, grinning.

"Don't take too much time," Kathy begged.

"Well-l, here's one—only it's supposed to be true," Larry began. "In 1845, Captain Andres Castillero came up from Baja California with private wealth and an adventuresome spirit. He was visiting in San Jose when he learned about a pit in the mountains a few miles from town where a reddish earth was being dug and then used for paint.

"He became very curious about the unusual dirt, and made a trip out to the mine to investigate. After examining the red ore carefully, he smelted a handful by putting it in his musket barrel over a fire. The soil that trickled out was quicksilver.

"Captain Castillero returned to town and immediately filed a claim to the area, and it was approved under the Mexican Mining Law. The mine, which was called the New Almaden mine, began operating and soon was the largest producer of quicksilver in the world."

"I wonder if there's any of that ore around here now," said Bob. "If there is, I'm changing from rock hounding to mining."

"Right now?" asked Kathy. "If so, count me out!" She yawned. "I'm going to bed. Good night, what's left of it," she said and walked slowly into her tent.

"I'm sleepy now, too," said Linda, "but I'm almost afraid to close my eyes for fear one of those thieves will sneak into the camp again."

"From now on," said Bob, "I think that one of us men should stand watch while the rest sleep."

"Right," Cactus agreed. "So long as we see 'em first, we'll be as safe as a rattler in a rock pile."

"I'll take first watch," Larry offered.

"Make mine the last one," said Cactus, "an' I'll scare up a mess o' flapjacks for breakfast."

"I heard that," came Kathy's voice. "I'm famished just thinking about them. Hurry up and go to bed!"

Linda, Kathy, Bob, and Cactus went to sleep and Larry settled down in front of the fire to stand guard. When the girls awakened, the aroma of crisp fried bacon greeted them.

"Um—that smells yummy, Cactus," said Kathy, jumping up. "Can I help you?"

The foreman smiled and said, "Nope. I'm an

ornery man when it comes to cookin', young lady, an' I need t' work solitary-like."

"In that case," said Kathy, "I'll never learn your cooking secrets."

"Why don't we practice for the gymkhana while we're waiting for breakfast?" Linda suggested. "We could really use a workout before we start out on the trail again."

"We sure could," said Larry. He grimaced. "At least I could!"

"All right, let's go," Bob said. "It'll keep my mind off those pancakes."

They saddled their horses and when all four were mounted, Linda said, "There's a smooth, grassy spot just beyond our camp. Let's ride over to it." She led off and soon they reached the practice ground.

The four horses walked in a large circle, following one another. Chica danced a little, and at one point started to break for the brush.

"Oh, no, you don't," said Linda, holding the filly firmly in line. "I was afraid you'd try to take off for the wide-open spaces. Too much trail riding has spoiled you."

She held up her hand to stop the others and said, "Let's try the walk, trot, and canter race. That ought to get the horses more in the mood for a game or two."

"That's a good idea," Bob agreed.

The riders lined up at one end of the ring-shaped field, walked to the other end, trotted back, then cantered across. With his usual speed, Rocket was an easy winner. Kathy kept to a slow lope and finished by trotting around the ring again.

Chica was making it plain she did not care about playing games this morning. The filly came in second in the race, but broke her walk gait with a few dancing steps.

"You're still thinking of your scare last night, I guess," Linda said.

"What's next?" Kathy asked.

"We could use rocks and set up a cloverleaf," said Larry. "That would give the horses some figure practice."

"Fine," Linda answered. "That's just what they need."

The boys put two big rocks six feet apart at the near side. The horses were to start through these. Out in the middle of the ring, they placed a couple of stones a good distance from each other but in a straight line. A fifth rock was laid considerably farther out, and centered between the others to make a cloverleaf.

It was a race against time, and the skill of the event was for a rider to circle around each rock from right to left and make the complete outline of the cloverleaf.

Larry started off on Gypsy, but went the wrong way, around the first rock. Bob made his formation correctly, but Rocket clicked his shoe twice against the stones.

If those were barrels, they would have gone over, Bob told himself.

Linda took Chica around the cloverleaf all right, but the filly capered at the far rock, losing time. Kathy had stayed out of the maneuver, merely trotting Patches around the ring.

"Try again, everybody!" Linda called.

She led Chica d'Oro through a couple of figure eights, which the filly performed with ease. Now Linda placed her hand on the palomino's neck and leaned down. "Please, baby, won't you *try* to make a perfect cloverleaf? I know you can do it."

The palomino nickered as she always did when her mistress spoke to her in this tone.

"I hope that meant yes," said Linda, leading the filly back for another try at the course. This time the golden horse responded perfectly, her skittishness over.

"Good girl!" Linda praised her, patting the horse affectionately.

She guided her to the side of the field and dismounted. Reaching into a saddlebag, Linda brought out a piece of sugar and handed it to Chica d'Oro as a reward.

Just then Linda noticed strange hoofprints which

led off through the brush. Presuming they had been made by the stranger who had come to camp the night before, she stooped to examine them.

A small leather case was lying on the ground near the tracks. Maybe there's some identification inside! Linda thought excitedly.

She picked up the case quickly and opened it. "Red hair!" Linda exclaimed.

The case was filled with it!

Stuffing the case into her pocket, Linda mounted and rode back to join the others. They had finished practicing and returned to the campfire.

She dismounted and ran to her friends. "Look!" she cried. "I've found a clue! It must have been dropped by the intruder last night."

Cactus held the case open, and the others stared in amazement.

"It *is* true that the thief at the Highway House left the hair on purpose to fool the police!" Linda continued excitedly. "I'm sure either Fallon or Hill is guilty!"

"It certainly looks that way," Bob said. "There's no identification on this. However, there may be fingerprints."

"Wrap this up right careful," said Cactus, handing the case back to Linda, "an' we'll give it to the first sheriff we run into."

Linda found a clean handkerchief, wrapped it around the case, and laid it in her saddlebag.

Coming back she said, "I guess I've earned some of your flapjacks, Cactus. After that let's follow those horseshoe prints."

"Come an' get it!" called Cactus, taking a big platter of fried bacon and hot fluffy pancakes off the fire. He had made sugar syrup to pour over them.

"Um-m-m," said Linda, "these are really delicious, Cactus."

The others agreed and finished the breakfast in a short time. The girls insisted upon cleaning up afterward.

"I'll give you no argument thar," Cactus drawled with a grin.

While the girls were at work, Bob and Larry went to see which direction the strange rider had taken. It coincided with the one Cactus Mac had picked out as perhaps leading to the horseshoe mark indicated on the map.

Linda was excited to hear this. "We're getting close to those thieves, I know we are! Let's ride!"

Cactus Mac and the boys broke camp, then they all mounted, eager for the chase.

After riding a short while, Bob suddenly exclaimed, "I see an interesting outcropping of rock. Maybe it's significant. I'll go over and take a look." He rode off the trail and examined the cliffside. "There's a cave here, a big one," he called.

The others followed him to the entrance of the large, dark cavern.

"It looks man-made," Linda observed as she rode up.

"I'm going to explore it," Bob said. "Wait here." He dismounted and snapped on his flashlight. "Be right back," he called, and entered the dark opening.

The others sat still, eagerly awaiting a report. The minutes went by and the four riders began to shift around nervously in their saddles. Suddenly, from the depths of the cave, they heard a muffled, indistinct cry.

"That's Bob!" Linda cried out, jumping from her horse and rushing into the cave.

Condor Attack 12

"Follow me!" Linda called as she disappeared into the dark mouth of the cave opening.

"Ground-hitch your horses," Cactus said to the others as they dismounted. "They'll stay." The three did this, then ran to the cave.

"Ow!" Cactus suddenly cried out as his forehead banged against the side of the stone entrance. He fell heavily to the ground, unconscious.

Kathy dropped to her knees beside him as Larry leaned over, concerned. "I'll take care of him," she said. "You go on and help Bob!" Larry nodded, and ran forward.

Kathy examined the foreman's head and noted a bad bruise just above his forehead. She raced to her saddlebag, took out the canteen, and quickly poured water onto a handkerchief. Kathy hurried back and held the cool cloth firmly on the swelling spot.

A few moments later Cactus opened his eyes. "Who hit me?" he asked.

"That stone wall," Kathy said, glancing toward the cave.

"I reckon I won't argue with that," the foreman said, gingerly feeling the sore spot. "Fine thing. That'll learn me to go pokin' around caves."

"You ought to rest for a while," Kathy said.

"All right," Cactus promised. "I'll just set here and clear my noggin. You go now and see what all the yellin' in thar was for."

"If you're sure you'll be all right," Kathy said, "I'll go, but I'll come right back." She snapped on her flashlight, entered the cave, and made her way through the large, damp outer chamber into the far cavern. As Kathy approached she heard her friends' voices.

Larry and Linda were sweeping the cavern walls with their strong flashlight beams. Bright pink crystals glittered in the light. Bob had begun to chip them away with a small pick.

"It's topaz," Kathy said excitedly as she joined them.

"How's Cactus?" Larry asked.

"Fine, but he has a nasty bruise. He's resting now."

"I'm sorry I scared you all," said Bob. "I guess I got carried away in my excitement." He continued to chip out pieces of the transparent pink rock.

"There was probably a big deposit here at one time," said Linda, "but most of it has been chiseled out."

"This is beautiful," Kathy said, holding a piece in her hand. "Many people think topaz is a yellow-colored gem, but pink and blue topaz are certainly the loveliest. Dad and I found some peach-colored crystals once. I can't wait until he sees this sample."

"Robert Rock Hound has done it again," said Larry. "You're a real gem, Bob!"

"At least I'm not a chiseler," Bob retorted.

Linda laughed. "I'm going to see how Cactus is," she said. "I'll get my tools—yours too, Larry."

"I'll come with you," Kathy said, joining her.

When the girls stepped outside the cave, they found Cactus seated in the sunshine. There was a large purple bruise on his head.

"Feel better now?" Kathy asked.

"Sure," the foreman drawled. "Feelin' fine. Just happen to be as wobbly on my pins as a day-old calf."

Linda told him about Bob's topaz find, then she asked, "Is there anything we can do for you?"

"Shucks, I'll be fit as a fiddle in a bit," he assured her. "You all go along on in now, an' do your pickin'. I'll just set here in the sun for a spell."

The girls took the tools from their saddlebags and

returned to the cavern. It was hard work hacking out the topaz, and the four companions kept at the job steadily without talking.

It seemed as though they had been picking for a long time when Bob announced, "Well, that's about all there is, I guess! No more treasure!"

The rock hounds closed and tied their tote bags and walked out into the bright noon sunshine. "Where's Cactus?" Linda exclaimed, looking puzzled. "He was right here when we left him."

"Cactus!" Kathy called. "Cactus!"

Bob had gone over to the horses. "Buck is gone, too," he said slowly. "That's funny. I thought Cactus wasn't feeling strong."

"Maybe he went for water," Larry suggested.

"There's plenty in the canteens," Bob said.

"If he intended to ride off any distance, it's odd he didn't call into the cave to let us know, or leave a note," said Linda. "Let's look around."

"Nothing here," Bob said after they had searched the area. "I hate to say this," he added seriously, "but I'm worried about Cactus. He must be very weak and in no shape to put up much resistance."

"Resistance?" Kathy asked, startled. "What do you think has happened to him, Bob?"

"Well," he replied, "there is a possibility he was captured!"

"The way Indian Charlie was?" Kathy asked.

"Let's search for Cactus right away," Linda urged.

Everyone hastily mounted up. But after riding a fair distance in all directions without spotting the foreman, the foursome returned to the cave mouth.

In glum silence, Linda and Kathy prepared lunch, which they and the boys ate listlessly. As they finished, a horseman came riding around the side of the surrounding brush. He wore a piece of brightly colored Indian blanket around his head, tied with a string of beads.

"Cactus!" Linda called happily, jumping up. "Where have you been?"

"Howdy," the foreman greeted them.

"We've been so worried about you," Kathy said, as the lanky man dismounted.

"Thar weren't nothin' to fret about," Cactus said. "That's why I left that thar note for you while I went visitin' the Injuns."

"What note?" Bob asked.

"Wal, goll-lee!" drawled Cactus, going over to a large rock. "Sure ain't thar now!" He picked up the stone. "Jumpin' Jaspers, Lookee here!" he said. "I guess a bird run off with my yellow paper."

Around the rock were scratchings made by the feet of a huge bird.

Larry shook his head in amazement. "That's *some* bird! But why would it steal the note?"

"Some birds just take bright things and hide 'em in their nests."

"What did the note say, Cactus?" Linda asked.

Cactus grinned. "I reckon you're wonderin' where I went skedaddlin'. Wal, while I was a-settin' here in the sun, an Injun fella come ridin' by, so I stopped him an' asked if he'd seen any strangers hereabouts," the foreman explained. "Nope, he hadn't. I asked him 'bout the territory, an' soon we was real friendly-like, an' he wanted to know about this purple egg settin' on my head. I rode with him back to his squaw, an' she put some red-man medicine made o' herbs on my noggin. I reckon it helped some, 'cause I feel frisky as a bronc."

"You'd better eat something," Linda suggested kindly.

"I ate at the Injun village," Cactus said. "Hominy and salt pork. Mighty tasty too. Wal folks, I feel like hittin' the trail again. Anyone want to join me?"

"Let's go!" Linda said, mounting Chica d'Oro.

The five companions started out again, riding between dark, bushy junipers and sweet-smelling greasewood trees. At a spot where jagged rocks flanked one side of their trail, Larry held up a hand for a stop.

"Look over there!" he said quietly. "The note thief!"

The others gazed in the direction he was pointing

and saw an enormous bird perched on a small pinnacle. The creature had a bare yellowish head and neck with traces of white on the wings.

"Looks like a bald-headed vulture to me," Kathy murmured, "except it's much bigger."

"It's a condor," Larry said in a quiet voice. "They're very rare, almost extinct. The only ones that still exist are in this area."

Silently and swiftly he dismounted and opened his camera case. "I'm going to try for a picture of him," he said.

Creeping slowly nearer, he took a few shots. Suddenly the huge bird spread its gigantic wings and with a rush of air took off.

"That wingspread must be ten feet across," Bob said in an awed voice.

"Look! There's his mate!" Larry said, indicating a large, dull-gray bird seated on a broad stone ledge. At sight of the riders, the female bird wheeled around and fluttered away, squawking harshly. Where she had been sitting contentedly lay four eggs the size of baseballs.

Larry quickly aimed his camera. Just as he snapped the shutter, a dark shadow fell over him.

"Look out!" Bob called to his friend, as the huge male condor swooped down.

Larry ran for Gypsy, jumped into the saddle, and followed the others at a fast pace. They rode rapidly for a short distance, then seeing that the bird had reversed its course and returned to the rocks, they reined up.

"Whew!" Kathy gasped breathlessly. "That was really scary. And to think that a bird could do that to us!"

Cactus had been gazing about as they rested.

"Seems to me like we're near that spot on the map you're looking for," he drawled. "This here country is gettin' mighty rocky!"

"Come on then!" Linda said excitedly.

The Old Sol group continued riding along the trail, which wound crookedly between huge boulders and steep, rocky planes. When they reached a high ridge, the rock hounds exclaimed over the scene spreading out before them.

"Absolutely gorgeous!" said Linda.

Deep ravines snaked along the rugged granite sides of the gorge below. The chaparral on the walls was grayish green, and the lush growth was dotted with red Indian paintbrush. The riders sat silent, their eyes sweeping over the broad panorama.

"Look!" Linda cried out suddenly. "I see it! A small, horseshoe-shaped canyon!"

Box Canyon Prisoners 13

Cactus Mac gazed down at the rock-rimmed gorge below and nodded his head enthusiastically. "By thunder, you spotted the canyon all right, Linda."

Kathy smiled at Linda. "You know, I could have stared at that horseshoe-shaped box canyon all day and never known it was anything more than a pretty green spot in this mountain of rocks."

"I can hardly wait to get down there and investigate," said Linda. "The trouble is, how?"

"It's a mighty long way off," said Cactus, stroking his chin.

"But not as the crow flies," added Bob as he peered intently at the canyon below.

"Well, there's always the condor express," Kathy put in dryly.

"No, thank you," Larry said, and added, "You

know, if we could approach that canyon from the back instead of going way around to that narrow entrance, it'd be a lot quicker."

"Sure would," agreed Cactus, "provided we could get down into the canyon from the back. Seems to me those sides are pretty steep."

"Let's give it a try anyway," begged Linda. "Our horses have slid down steep mountainsides before."

"That's okay with me," said Bob. "And if we can't make it, we'll just have to take more time riding around from here to the entrance."

Linda grasped her reins tightly. "You lead the way, Cactus—and make it a short one."

Cactus Mac grinned. "I'll make it short's I can an' still keep it safe. Watch out for your hosses so they don't cut their pasterns on the rocky ridges."

It was a slow, rugged ride downward to the back of the little horseshoe canyon, but by careful maneuvering the group made it without any mishaps. Cactus slowly surveyed the canyon sides.

"Too steep for the hosses, I'm 'fraid," he declared with finality.

"*We* could slide down, though," Linda put in.

"Sure, why not?" Bob agreed. "We can tie our horses right here."

"And just how do you figger you'll get back up?" asked Cactus, a smile playing over his features.

"Same way we go down, only in reverse," Linda answered impishly.

Cactus shook his head. "You could no more climb up those steep, silty sides'n shinny up a greased pole!"

"I'll meet you at the entrance the long way 'round," said Kathy. "Giddy-ap, Patches!"

"Whoa there, gal!" said Cactus. "I've no mind to slide into that canyon myself, but you kids can get all the slidin' you want. I'll put the hosses on a string, go on 'round, an' bring 'em to you through the entrance. By that time you should've figgered out what's bottled up down there."

"All right, Cactus," agreed Linda. "But won't four horses be too many to keep in one line?"

"Wal, now," the foreman drawled, his eyes crinkling at the corners, "thar was a time when I made it 'cross the Bitterroot Mountains up in Montana with a string o' twenty—headed for a gold strike where I aimed to sell 'em." He chuckled. "Made more on them critters than if I'd'a spent two years diggin' for dust!"

The boys promptly fixed the horses on the line. Linda patted Chica d'Oro reassuringly. "Be a good baby, now."

The palomino nickered, but had a somewhat bewildered look in her eyes.

"Do you think she'll be all right, Cactus?" Linda asked with concern. "I'd rather never know what's in this canyon than have anything happen to Chica."

"Don't be frettin'," replied Cactus. "Even wildies go along all right on a string. They kinda like followin' one 'nother."

Each young rock hound took out a digging tool, then the ranch foreman started off. Chica d'Oro made surefooted progress, seemingly enjoying her adventure without the extra weight of a rider.

Linda was the first one over the canyon side, and with the others slid down the silty, rock-strewn wall. The four stumbled and collided at the bottom amid gales of laughter.

"Whew!" gasped Larry, brushing himself off. "Now that's what I call a shortcut!"

Linda quickly took in the scene. "It's terribly quiet and untouched-looking here," she murmured, "almost as if no one's ever dug in this spot." She took a deep breath. "Where shall we begin our search?" she asked, impatient to get started. "There are no pits, so if there are any turquoise deposits, they haven't been disturbed."

Bob pointed to a hump of rocks near the other side of the canyon. "If there is any turquoise here, it's my guess that we've found the spot."

The four young people walked the short distance over the hard-packed dirt floor of the canyon to examine the formation. "Doesn't look as if anyone's been chiseling at these," stated Bob, running his fingers over the rough, hard surface.

"Then this *must* be where the unclaimed turquoise deposit is," said Linda triumphantly.

Eagerly the rock hounds started chipping at the rocks. It was slow, tedious work, but suddenly Linda exclaimed, "I've found some turquoise!"

The others gathered around her and looked in awe at the blue-studded rock she held up. Kathy was ecstatic. "That's it all right! We've found the untapped mine!"

Linda grabbed her friends and they did an impromptu dance to celebrate their find.

"It's a fabulous reward!" exulted Bob, and Larry wore an ear-to-ear grin.

"Wait until Cactus Mac sees this!" Linda cried.

"We're going to need our other tools in order to do any more work," Larry said. "Let's walk down toward the entrance and see if Cactus has arrived yet."

At that precise moment, a strange, drawn-out sound echoed across the canyon. It sounded like "K-e-e-p o-u-t! T-u-r-n- b-a-c-k!"

The four stopped frozen in their tracks and waited tensely.

"What was that?" cried Kathy, barely moving a muscle.

"Maybe a strange bird or animal?" put in Larry. "Could be a cougar. They can scream just like a person."

"It sounded more like a human voice to me," Linda said. "Hide your digging tools!"

Suddenly the weird sound came again. "G-e-t o-u-t! G-e-t o-u-t! Run for your lives!"

"We'd better do it!" said Kathy, starting to run toward the entrance to the box canyon.

The others followed quickly, and Linda suggested that in any case they must not give away their secret. The sound was not repeated. Reaching the entrance the group looked for their trail boss but saw no sign of him.

"That's odd," said Kathy. "We should be able to spot Cactus and the string of horses a long way off."

"Looking for someone, girlie?" suddenly asked a rude, harsh voice.

The young people wheeled to face four masked men. Black cloth hoods completely disguised their identities. They moved stealthily to surround the Craigs and their friends. As they did, Linda noted a large, covered horse van attached to a car at the left side of the entrance.

The harsh voice spoke again. "I shouted a warning to you to get out of here. But no, you had to start snooping around these rocks. This place belongs to us. You got no right to be in this canyon, and we're going to see that you're taken far away from it." He backed up his remarks by patting his holster.

The young people waited, tense and uncertain. Where was Cactus Mac? What could they do to stall for time?

"Into the van, all of you, and pronto!" snapped the man. He motioned a burly arm toward the waiting vehicle. "Don't make us force you with a weapon."

The ramp door was swung down by one of the other men, and the young people were roughly pushed inside. Then the door was swung shut and they heard the click of a heavy lock.

Kathy slumped down on the floor of the truck. "Well, this is great, just great," she said, a quaver in her voice. "Just who do these men think they are, and what do they have against us?"

The four captives looked at one another dejectedly, and Linda sighed. "I have a pretty good idea *who* they are—and chances are they're after exactly what we were after!"

"The turquoise deposit?" Kathy guessed.

"Right."

"There must be a way to escape from these guys and get help," said Bob, still angry that he had not dared fight these ruffians.

"We must keep watching for our big chance," said Larry.

The van creaked and rattled over a bumpy road, jostling its passengers about. "Where do you suppose they're taking us?" asked Linda, trying to keep from bumping into her friends.

"Probably away to some deep, dark pit," Kathy muttered.

Bob spoke with more bravado than he actually felt. "Don't worry, Kathy, we'll get out somehow."

Presently their vehicle jolted to a stop. The door was let down and the four occupants ordered out. Instantly the ramp was swung upward again. Linda and her companions found themselves in a small, open area with high, perpendicular rock walls on all sides. The entrance to it was a narrow crevice which was blocked completely by the van.

"It's a box canyon," Larry noted grimly.

Linda's eyes searched the shadowy spot. "Look! Our horses!" she exclaimed suddenly. "But Cactus Mac and Buck aren't here!"

Bob addressed the masked men. "What has happened to our foreman?" he demanded.

"Now wouldn't you like to know!" asked a raspy voice. It was followed by a menacing laugh.

"I'll bet he escaped," said Kathy, "and he'll get us out of here!"

"Ha! He'd have to be a magician to escape from where he was put!" another man told them.

Linda was fearful for Cactus. He too was a prisoner! "What's the idea of holding us here?" she demanded.

"Well, I'll tell you," replied the tallest man of the group. "We have some turquoise prospecting to do and we don't want any young punks to get in our way."

Linda's pulse quickened. She was sure this was Fallon trying to disguise his voice!

"Why don't you just go do your digging and leave us here?" asked Larry.

"We'll go when we're ready," rasped another man, "and you'll be left, all right."

"What did he mean by that?" Kathy whispered to her friends. "Take our horses and leave us stranded?"

"Oh, no!" Linda murmured. "Not Chica—he's not going to take *her*!"

"We must try to outsmart them, that's vital," said Bob. "One thing I'm sure of—they're not just going to drive off and let us escape."

Linda nodded and, moving nearer the men, watched them cautiously. She carefully regarded the tall, thin man who was presently remaining in the background. Finally she saw the clue to his identity—the brown agate ring!

Linda spoke boldly. "You may as well unmask, Mr. Fallon. We know who you are. And you, too, Mr. Hill," she said to his shorter companion.

The men were visibly startled but gave no affirmative answer. "You must have someone else in mind," said the one accused of being Fallon. "We don't answer to those names."

Linda hesitated for a moment, then decided not to mention her clue to his identity. That would be something for the law to tackle. If Fallon should remove the ring, the evidence would be lost.

Instead, she persisted with her accusations. "You are Fallon and Hill, and you're wanted by the New York police for passing bad checks. Do you deny that?" Bob gave her an encouraging nod.

The two men said nothing. Their two henchmen uttered a few guttural words, and the one with the harsh voice blurted out, "You know too much, and you'll regret it!" Linda and her friends exchanged significant glances.

How are we going to escape from this trap? Linda wondered anxiously.

The four thieves went into huddled conversation beside their car. Linda stealthily walked to a position at the front where she would be concealed from the men yet able to hear them speak.

"The boss said he'd cut us all in for a good share if we found the turquoise deposit," said one. "The rest of you remember that, in case he backs down."

"He won't. He'll have plenty of cash," Hill replied. "He's got that same rich buyer waiting for the turquoise—the one who bought those garnets."

"Yes, and he's going to pay a big price for that Persian turquoise," said Fallon.

Linda drew in her breath sharply. Fallon must still have the valuable, old Persian gem!

"It's going to be a big job chiseling out the

turquoise deposit here," the burly ruffian pointed out.

"That's what we cut you two in for," Fallon said. "I'm no rock prospector. I'm the contact man. You bragged you were experts on rocks!"

"Sure we are," retorted a raspy voice. "We'll get the stuff out all right, if you make the job worth our while."

"You'll get your cut," Hill replied angrily. "Just be patient."

"Why don't we get on now with our excavatin'?" the burly stranger asked impatiently. "That's what we came to do."

"We can't go until it's darker," replied Fallon. "We're too close to a big thing to have a chance rider spot us and pull the law on our trail. That would really mess up all our plans."

As the men started to separate, Linda quickly made her way back to her companions.

"This gang are members of a professional jewel thieves' ring," she said in a low voice, repeating all she had heard the men say.

Bob spoke up. "As long as that van is blocking the entrance, escape for us is impossible. We'll just have to sit tight until the men pull out tonight."

"And even then they may post a guard over us," Larry added in a discouraged tone. "It may be a month before we're released!"

Escape Signals 14

Disconsolate, Linda and the others moved over to the horses. "They look all right," she observed, stroking Chica d'Oro. "Are you okay, baby?"

Chica responded with an unenthusiastic nicker, as if sensing the depressed spirits of the captives.

Kathy said wryly, "That's just the way I feel—all right, but not happy about our predicament."

Meanwhile Bob had stealthily checked their equipment. "At least," he murmured, "the crooks didn't take our topaz."

Larry spoke up. "They probably don't think it's worth anything," he reasoned. "They're waiting to remove the valuable turquoise from the horseshoe canyon deposit."

Linda, her eyes troubled, said, "If we don't escape tonight, and Cactus Mac is held prisoner someplace, what will happen to our packhorses back at camp?"

"I believe they'll be okay for a while," Bob said comfortingly. "We gave them extra water and pellet food this morning. Also, they're on long enough ropes to reach and forage on the brush and ground stuff."

Linda seethed under the forced captivity for another reason. "Our gymkhana practice was wasted," she remarked, looking at her friends who also wore downcast expressions. "We'll never make the Alpha Ranch gymkhana in time!"

A moment later the young rider's face took on a determined look. "Let's stop moping and figure a plan of escape. The first step is to find out exactly where we are. Maybe the map will help."

"Right, Sis," Bob agreed, and Linda furtively slipped the map from under her jacket. The others clustered around her to peruse it.

So deep were they in concentration that the foursome did not hear the sound of approaching footsteps. Suddenly Hill forced his way among them and grabbed the map from Linda's hands.

"I'll take this now," he snarled. "It's mine."

"Prove it!" Linda retorted, facing him squarely. "How do we know it belongs to you?"

The man sneered. "I'll tell you how it's mine," he said gloatingly. "I paid a lot of money for this map. Bought it from an old Indian whose people knew about the turquoise deposit. I hid it in my saddle." Hill's eyes narrowed menacingly at the four young people. "You stole my horse and the map."

"That's not true!" Linda blazed. "You've seen all our horses. You know very well there isn't a strange one among them!"

For a moment Hill looked blank at being caught in the falsehood. Then he glared at Linda. "None of your smart lip, girlie."

Undaunted, she countered, "Was it you and Mr. Fallon who came sneaking into our camp a couple of times?"

Hill swaggered a little. "Sure. We knew you had the map and that it showed a valuable turquoise deposit. We aimed to get that map." He gave her a short, unpleasant laugh. "And now we've succeeded."

"How did you find out we had it?" Linda demanded.

A smirk curled Hill's lips. "You'd like me to tell you, wouldn't you?" he asked. "Well, maybe I'll be real generous and do just that, since you won't be getting out of here for a long time." He paused, then added threateningly, "Maybe never."

Bob restrained a strong impulse to crack his fist against the man's jaw. Gritting his teeth, the boy snapped, "Get on with the story."

"Sure, sure," was the taunting reply. "We met your friends Warner and Becker on the trail after you'd seen them. They asked us if we knew of an odd horseshoe-shaped pit or canyon marked on an old map of this area. We told them we didn't, but friendly-like asked them to tell us all about it."

Hill gave a smug chuckle. "They figured we were pals of yours and gave us all the details. When we didn't have any luck getting the map, we decided to trail you till we did, or till you located the horseshoe area containing the turquoise."

Fallon came over and added, "This time we've caught up with you, all right."

Linda ignored the remark and said, "You didn't know about the map the first night you came into our camp after the cloudburst. What were you looking for then?"

Fallon answered readily. "We knew that girl" —he pointed to Kathy—"is Hamilton's kid, and if she was out rock-hounding she'd have an ultraviolet light. That's what we wanted."

"It's hanging right there on her saddle," said Hill. "Guess I'll help myself." He sauntered over to Patches and began to untie the light from the saddle strings.

"Don't you dare!" cried Kathy, forgetting her fear for the moment. She started toward the man, but Bob took her arm and gently pulled her back.

"Better not antagonize these fellows," he cautioned in a whisper. "They're winning now, but our turn will come."

Meantime Fallon had joined his pal, and the two unfastened the picks tied to the horses' saddles.

"These'll come in mighty handy, too," said Hill with another smirk.

The prisoners stood by in silent dismay as the thieves continued to help themselves to the young people's equipment. Bob groaned inwardly when Hill reached out for the two-way radio strapped to the cantle of Rocket's saddle. The man gave a triumphant snort. "We sure won't leave *this* for you to use and bring lawmen on our necks before we clear out of here for good."

There goes our main hope for rescue, thought Linda dejectedly.

Finally Fallon and Hill turned toward the foursome. "You stay put right here with your horses," Hill warned, "and don't try giving us any trouble. We wouldn't like that. Understand?"

Snickering in satisfaction, he and his companion strode back to the car with their loot. The Craigs and their friends temporarily put aside thoughts of their plight to care for the horses. The animals had been tied up close to a tall, dead mesquite.

"We might as well unsaddle them," Linda said, "since we won't be riding for a while."

After this was done, the horses were given long tie ropes and placed far enough apart so that each would have enough space in which to graze amid the ground cover.

Once more the captives discussed in low tones possible means of escape, while keeping watchful eyes on the men who stood in front of their car.

"I'm tempted to sneak past them and run like a hurricane for help," Larry said.

"You wouldn't get far with a bullet in your back," Bob stated flatly.

"Don't I know it," Larry admitted ruefully.

Linda again glanced toward the car. "The men have gone out of sight," she noted. "Maybe they're taking a siesta,"

"Not at the same time," Larry said. "One would stay on guard."

Linda nodded thoughtfully, gazing at a huge pile of rocks near the van. "I'm going to climb those rocks," she declared, "and see if I can find out where they are. I have an idea on how to get help."

Quickly she pulled off her boots and before anyone could stop her, moved silently away on hands and knees. The boys and Kathy watched tensely, fearful that one of the men would spot her.

Finally Linda reached the pile of rocks and crept nimbly up them to the top. Peering down, she saw Fallon, Hill, and their pals seated before a small fire about fifty yards away. The men were intent on heating a pot of coffee and opening cans of food.

Good! thought Linda.

Cautiously but rapidly she returned to the others. "They're eating," she said. "Now's our chance!"

"Chance for what?" Kathy asked. "Something to do with your idea?"

"Yes." Linda turned to her brother. "My plan will require the sacrifice of your gorgeous shirt."

"My *shirt*!" Bob echoed, mystified. "Well, sure, Sis. But don't tell me you're going to use it as a signal flag. Those crooks would spot it in a second."

Despite the seriousness of the situation, everyone had to grin. "You're telling me!" Larry said. "That bright pink with the black zigzag lines could be seen from here to Old Sol!"

"Exactly." Linda went on to explain what she had in mind. "If you'll tear out the sleeves, Bob, I'll tie some horsehairs around them and fasten the sleeves through the eyes that hold the ramp chains. Someone *might* recognize the unique shirt design, or at least wonder about the horsehairs enough to notify the police."

"A long chance," Bob said, "but it could work. Let's try it."

In case any of their captors might suddenly come upon them, Bob pretended to be suffering from the heat as he removed his shirt. Then, with Larry and Kathy shielding him, he ripped out the sleeves. Linda, meanwhile, deftly removed several hairs from Rocket's black tail and a dozen from Chica's white one.

Quickly the hairs were wound about the sleeves. Linda took these and, keeping alert, made her way noiselessly to the van. She paused long enough to be sure the men had not returned, then fastened one sleeve to each eye, securing them tightly.

Surely the driver will stop sometime for fuel and water, Linda reasoned, and perhaps my strange signal will be noticed by a service attendant.

Suddenly she heard a slight noise behind her and whirled. To her intense relief and amazement, the person was Larry. He passed her and went to crouch by the left rear wheel of the car. He began to slash at the tread with a sharp rock.

Linda ran over to him. "Good work! That should help put a kink in their scheme!"

"Sure hope so," said Larry tersely. "Say, you did a swell job. Very clever."

Without further delay, the two plotters hurried back to the others. Kathy and Bob greeted them with sighs of relief and praise for their success.

"You're both phenomenal," said Kathy.

"Thanks." Linda smiled. "What I really am right now is thirsty. I know we should conserve the water in our canteens, but I could certainly use a drop."

Bob promptly handed his over and insisted that his sister and Larry take generous sips. "That's the least I can offer you," he said.

Linda gave a little chuckle. "Well, Brother, if your shirt does the trick, I won't ask for anything else—for a while."

The young people began a tense vigil, hoping that their captors would not notice the sleeves attached to the van. Fortunately it was growing dusky, muting their bright color.

Finally the four men reappeared. As they strode past the van, Linda and the others held their breath. But the thieves hurried on and came directly up to the prisoners.

"We're taking off," Fallon told them curtly, and Hill added with a sneer, "Make yourselves at home—there's nothing else you can do. No chance to escape."

"No, I guess there isn't," Linda replied as if in resignation. "But before you leave, there are a few things I'd like to know. Did you two steal the garnets from Mr. Hamilton?"

"Sure we did," was Hill's boastful reply. "We're in the gem business too, remember?"

"But hardly running an honest company," Linda retorted. She pursued her questioning. "No doubt you left the mud and the red hairs to fool us."

"That's right," said Fallon. "We're a smart pair to beat. We've got the law and you young punks just where we want you."

"Come on," one of the other men prodded. "Let's get out of here!"

The thieves started off. Hill, however, stopped them suddenly and turned around. With a sardonic laugh he said to the captives, "I almost forgot to tell you something else. You all better move real fast to the far side of the canyon."

"Why?" Bob asked.

"Because," replied Hill with obvious relish, "we're going to seal the entrance with a blast of dynamite."

A chill went down Linda's spine. The next moment Bob and Larry hurled themselves furiously on the four men. The boys' fists lashed out in all directions. Two of their adversaries fell back from the surprise onslaught, but instantly the others' hands flew to their holsters.

"Enough funny stuff!" Fallon barked.

He and his partners stalked to their car, climbed in, and roared off. Bob and Larry clenched their fists, white-faced with anger.

"I'm sure those men meant what they said," Linda declared. "We'd better race to the other side before they set off the dynamite."

"Those low-down desert rats!" Bob hissed. "Wish we could have slugged them for keeps."

With feverish haste the rock hounds untied the horses and led them to the far side of the canyon. Linda and the others stood by their animals, grimly awaiting the sound of an explosion.

"Sorry I got you into such a mess, baby," Linda murmured, stroking Chica d'Oro. "Our only hope," she added fervently, "is for somebody to notice the signals on that van!"

Before anyone could comment, there came a deafening *boo-oo-om* which shook the ground.

The Craigs and their friends stared at one another wordlessly. Hill had told the truth. Escape was cut off!

Gymkhana Challenge   15

For the past several hours Cactus Mac, a prisoner in an abandoned mine tunnel, had been struggling to free himself from his bonds. The foreman was bound to an iron ring bolted into the rock.

"Drat those masked hombres what did this!" he murmured.

His horse, a beautiful buckskin, stood patiently at the entrance, watching the gyrations of his master with puzzled eyes.

"By cracky, Buck!" Cactus exclaimed. "She's givin' way. A few more tries, an' I'll be out o' this dungeon."

He looked fondly at the big horse. "I'm sure glad you stuck with me, old pal. What those varmints don't know 'bout hosses'd fill a book."

The men had turned Buck loose. But the horse had not gone off, remaining instead out of sight behind a huge rocky projection covered with brush.

As soon as the men had gone off, Cactus had whistled. Buck, hearing the familiar sound, had galloped to the tunnel entrance and stood there ever since.

Cactus rested from his efforts and squinted out into the fading daylight. Yup, he thought with satisfaction, them ornery crooks pounded me with a lot o' questions 'bout that thar map, but I didn't tell 'em a thing.

The foreman frowned. But I'm a-wonderin' what's happened to the young folks. If they've run into them sidewinders. . . .

The thought gave Cactus renewed strength. He took a deep breath and strained with all his might away from the iron ring. There was a grinding, rasping sound as the bolt suddenly pulled loose from the rock wall. The wiry man went hurtling forward, but finally came to a stop, still on his feet.

"Glory be!" he gasped. "I made it!"

He shook the rope which still bound his hands behind him. "Now to get out o' *this* contraption!"

Cactus ducked his head to his shirt pocket, and with his teeth pulled out a book of matches. He dropped them to the ground, then hunkered down on his heels so the matches were behind him. He managed to reach the book with his fingers, extract a match, and light it, firing the pack.

The foreman held his tied wrists above the flame

and smiled as he felt the strands loosen. In another moment the rope gave way completely. Cactus leaped toward Buck and swung into the saddle.

"We got to travel fast, Buck," he said, "to notify the sheriff an' catch up with them vipers."

With a practiced eye, Cactus Mac studied his surroundings. "Thar's ranch country near here," he muttered. "Come on, old boy, git a move on!"

Buck and his rider sped off at a full gallop along the mountainous road. Reaching a crest, Cactus pulled up short. Below him, parked at the side of the road, was a car and horse van. One rear tire on the automobile was flat. Two men were changing it, while four others stood watching.

But it was not the flat tire that drew Cactus's special attention. The foreman could distinguish two pieces of material hanging from the van.

Curious, Cactus turned Buck around and rode to a spot out of sight of the car. He ground-hitched the horse, then stealthily crept through the thick brush alongside the road. Cactus stopped at a point several yards from the van and cautiously peered out.

He almost cried aloud in astonishment. "Them's pink sleeves tied on that! They got zigzags—black ones—like Bob's shirt! And sure as shootin' they been put on with hairs from the tails o' Chica d'Oro and Rocket!"

In a moment the foreman realized that the Craigs and their friends must be prisoners, but somehow had managed to send out this SOS, which apparently had not been noticed by the men.

Two o' them fellas are the ones what trussed me up! Cactus told himself excitedly. The rest must have got Linda and Bob and their pals!

The foreman scrambled back to Buck, jumped into the saddle, and sent the big buckskin on a run to the nearest ranch house. Hastily Cactus dismounted and pounded on the door impatiently.

A startled woman answered. "What's the matter?"

"Please, ma'am, may I use your phone?" Cactus gasped. "Got to call the sheriff. Whar's the nearest town?"

"Ruddville."

The woman indicated a table telephone in the hallway. Cactus Mac snatched up the receiver and called Deputy Sheriff Wilkins. When the officer heard Cactus's story, he said briskly, "I'll bring men and get right over to the truck. Meet you there!"

Cactus thanked the woman and dashed outside. He leaped into the saddle and Buck galloped off. They reached the car and van at the same time Wilkins and three deputies drove up from the opposite direction. The lawmen parked crosswise, blocking the road, and jumped out.

The tire had been changed and the car engine

was racing, but the car was surrounded and the occupants were ordered to alight.

Sullenly they obeyed. Cactus Mac had dismounted and run up to confront them. Two of the men blanched upon seeing the foreman. One blurted, "How did you get—" and broke off, biting his lip.

"How'd I get free?" Cactus snapped. "I managed." He turned to Wilkins. "These fellas belong to the masked gang what tied me up. Them sleeves on the van belong to Bob Craig's shirt. The tail hairs are from his hoss and Linda's. The Craigs an' two o' their friends are prisoners someplace an' these no-good critters know whar."

Meanwhile the deputies had searched the rear of the car and found various tools and rock-hound equipment, including an ultraviolet lamp.

"Okay, you!" Wilkins barked to the suspects. "Start talking!"

The men were stubbornly silent at first, but after being handcuffed and questioned further they admitted to having captured the Craigs and their companions. When Cactus learned that two of the men were named Fallon and Hill, he cried:

"I think they're gem thieves—the ones what broke into Mr. Hamilton's shop." He whirled on Hill, who glared at him balefully. "You lead us to the young 'uns, pronto!"

Wilkins gave brisk orders. The van was to be unhooked. Two of his deputies were to drive the car, while he and the third officer would take the prisoners in the police car. "Cactus, you trail along on horseback."

Under Fallon's reluctant guidance, the procession presently reached the blocked-up entrance to the box canyon. The deputies and their prisoners piled out. Cactus Mac rode up a few minutes later.

"Your rock hounds are inside." Hill pointed toward the canyon, then sneered. "We fixed up the entrance with dynamite!"

"Dynamite!" Cactus Mac cried out furiously. "Why you—!"

"Don't worry," muttered Hill. "We warned those kids to move out of the way."

Deputy Sheriff Wilkins fixed the man with a steely look. "You and your pals will break a way through those rocks," he commanded, and directed his assistants to bring out the pickaxes from the car.

"Okay!" he barked. "Get to work!"

Not only the prisoners, but Cactus Mac and the officers set to work hacking at the barrier of rocks and rubble. When a narrow opening had been chipped halfway through, Fallon dropped his pickax, complaining, "Can't do another stroke. My hands are full of blisters."

A deputy brandished a gun. "Back to work!"

Scowling, Fallon complied, and the backbreaking job progressed without further interruption. Cactus

Mac, perspiration streaming down his face, wielded his pickax with grim-faced determination.

At this point, the Craigs and their friends were resting against their saddles at the far end of the canyon. Although weary, the discouraged foursome were finding it difficult to sleep. They had partaken sparingly of their dwindling rations and water.

Earlier, Larry had suggested that they try to climb over the high barrier of rocks, but this idea had been overruled. No one wished to leave the horses unattended. Besides, it was possible the gang had left an armed guard in the event of an attempted escape.

Suddenly Linda sat bold upright. Were her ears deceiving her, or did they detect a metallic sound— as of steel ringing against rock? She awakened Bob and the others from their fitful slumber, and the four sprang up. They listened intently as the sound was repeated. It came from the sealed-off canyon entrance.

"Pickaxes!" Bob exclaimed. "Let's hope they're in the hands of friends!"

By now the horses were whinnying in excitement, their ears pricked forward.

"We'll soon find out," Larry said as the hacking noise steadily drew closer.

Tensely the young captives shone flashlights on the rocky barrier. Just when the suspense of waiting became almost unbearable, they saw a small wedge open up between two boulders and a familiar face peer through the opening.

"Cactus Mac!" shouted Linda and Bob. With Kathy and Larry they raced toward the foreman.

Cactus scrambled through the hole he had opened with his pick and flung the tool aside. "Praise be!" he greeted them joyously. "You're okay!"

"We are now!" Bob grinned.

By this time the cleft between the rocks had been widened by the other men. Deputy Sheriff Wilkins stepped through it and came up to the group.

Linda and the others listened intently as Cactus related his own experience and his spotting of the sleeve signals on the thieves' van.

Linda turned gratefully to Larry. "When you caused that flat tire you really saved the day."

Larry chuckled. "I'd say good teamwork did the trick."

The three deputies leading the prisoners, now handcuffed, joined the others. Fallon, Hill, and their partners scowled upon seeing the rock hounds. Linda handed Wilkins the leather case filled with red hair, then related the conversation she had overheard about the garnets' being sold.

She looked squarely at Fallon and asked, "Where is the Persian turquoise you stole from Mr. Hamilton's shop?"

The thief denied knowing anything about the

valuable stone. But Linda had noticed his hand touch a jacket pocket and brought this to the deputy sheriff's attention.

Wilkins immediately ordered that the man be searched. This was quickly done by a deputy, who plucked a small flannel bag from Fallon's pocket. He handed it to Kathy, saying, "Perhaps you'd like to open this."

With trembling fingers, Kathy untied the string on the little pouch and withdrew an opaque, green, hexagonal-shaped stone.

"The Persian turquoise!" she gasped happily. "Oh, Dad will be so thrilled!"

The map showing the horseshoe canyon was found in Hill's possession. Wilkins handed it to Linda.

The party then prepared to leave. The aperture hacked through the rocks was barely wide enough to accommodate the horses. The officers, guarding the captured thieves, went first, followed by Cactus and the young people, who led their mounts.

"Baby," murmured Linda to Chica as the palomino picked her way along surefootedly, "we're on our way home at last!"

They finally reached the two cars, where Buck stood waiting.

Kathy suddenly gave a tremendous sigh of relief. "I hope I never have to make another trip like this one!" she said.

Linda nodded, then remarked, "I still feel bad that we can't get back in time for the Alpha Ranch gymkhana tomorrow!"

"You expected to ride in it?" asked Wilkins.

"Yes."

"Don't worry," he assured her. "I'll radio to Ruddville right now for vans."

"Wonderful!" Linda cried. "Oh, thank you!"

The deputy sheriff put in the call over the two-way radio in his car, then said, "They'll get 'em here as soon as possible."

Cactus Mac rode off, saying he would get the three packhorses from the campsite. Shortly after he returned, two large horse vans arrived.

Just before Chica d'Oro was led into one of them, Linda pulled Kathy aside, put something into her hand, and whispered a message.

"Okay," Kathy said in a low voice. "I'll do it as soon as we get back."

The return trip was made without incident. Kathy and Larry were dropped off at their homes, and the Craigs and Cactus Mac went on to Old Sol. Linda and Bob, exhausted, tumbled into bed as soon as they had told all their news to Doña and Bronco. The Mallorys, astounded, praised their grandchildren highly for bringing the gemstone mystery to a successful conclusion.

Next morning Linda and her brother awoke refreshed and ready for the gymkhana. After breakfast they quickly fed and groomed the horses. Linda was glad to note that Chica d'Oro seemed full of pep.

"You'll need all your energy for the games," she said, patting the filly.

The Craigs made a quick trip to the Highway House to offer Mr. Hamilton the map of Horseshoe Canyon. They were greeted by a smiling Kathy. She led them to her father's shop, where he welcomed Linda and Bob with a broad grin.

"I don't know how to thank you all for retrieving this treasure," he said, holding up the precious green turquoise.

"It's just too good to be true!" added Mrs. Hamilton as she entered the room. "Oh, it's such a relief to know that those awful thieves are in jail."

Linda's eyes sparkled. She took the old map from her pocket and handed it to Mr. Hamilton. "We think you should have this," she said, and pointed out the area where they had located the turquoise deposit.

"Splendid!" he exclaimed. "I'll take a trip up there first chance I get."

Linda looked at her watch. "It's time we were leaving for the Alpha Ranch," she reminded the others.

"Right," said Bob. "Let's go!"

Before they departed, Kathy winked at Linda and murmured, "Dad will start on it right away."

"Oh, good," Linda whispered.

Back at Old Sol, the brother and sister found Larry waiting for them. As soon as Kathy rode up on Patches, the four set off.

Arriving at the Alpha Ranch, they found that a large crowd of spectators and contestants had already gathered. A big pit barbecue and snack booths added to the air of excitement. The best riders from miles around were there, Linda noted.

"I hope I can win that Mexican Ring Spearing today," she confided to her brother.

"That takes the peak of skill," he said. "You're going to have some expert competition."

"I know," Linda agreed. "I'll just concentrate hard on winning."

"I'll bet on you," Larry assured her.

Kathy spoke up determinedly. "And I'll go all out to win the Musical Stalls."

Soon the games got under way. Kathy won first place in her favorite event and was roundly cheered. Bob placed first in the Pole Bending, and Larry in the Keyhole Race. Linda won the Walk, Trot, and Canter Race.

They all placed in several of the other games they entered, except Kathy, who was content with her one triumph. Linda was conserving Chica d'Oro for the Mexican Ring Spearing, the last event.

There were only five entries for this game— Linda and four boys. Few riders had become expert enough at this competition to try it in a big show. One of the boys was Vance Martin, slim, dark, and rather arrogant. He and his Arabian had won a good many of the contests.

I'll have to watch him, thought Linda.

Standing near the horse entry gate was a lad of about twelve. He said cockily in a loud voice, "My brother Vance will win this—wait and see!"

Vance, astride his horse, had a superior expression on his face. Linda, observing him, thought, He certainly looks as if he expects to win easily.

She bent over in her saddle and murmured to Chica d'Oro, "We'll see about that, won't we, baby?" The filly responded with a low nicker.

The setup for the spearing event was two lines of four poles with an extended arm on each one, from which hung a ring. The riders, holding wands, were to canter down one side picking off the rings, turn at the end, and canter back along the other side, again snatching rings.

It will be fun but hard, thought Linda.

The shortest elapsed time and the greatest number of rings on a rider's wand were the determining factors for victory.

Linda spoke to her palomino. "This depends as much on you as on me. Let's go!"

The entrants drew numbers for performing positions. Linda was fifth and Vance Martin second. He picked off and retained all of the rings on his wand.

Kathy, Bob, and Larry, watching tensely, heard people around them comment that young Martin would probably win the event.

Linda had noticed how Vance slowed slightly at each post in order to be sure of spearing his ring. I can beat him on time, she told herself. Now if I can just pick off all the rings!

The other three contestants had lost two or more rings and were eliminated. When Linda was handed her wand, she hesitated for one moment at the starting line and took a deep breath. Then she gave Chica the go signal.

With her eyes fixed on the rings, she neatly picked off the first two with obviously better speed than Vance Martin. Chica made the turn at the end without the need of a signal.

Linda came back smoothly along the second row of posts. One by one she picked off the rings, retaining them all on her wand. The applause of the crowd was tremendous.

Then, just as she spurted the last twenty feet to the finish line, something sharp struck her hand. The pain caused Linda to dip her wand, and half the rings slid off just before she crossed the line. The audience sat in stunned silence, while Linda grasped her hand in utter bewilderment.

"What's the matter, Miss Craig?" asked one of the judges.

"Some-something hit my hand," replied Linda,

revealing a bright red mark on her skin. "It felt like a stone."

A little pigtailed girl ran up to the judges' box. "I know what happened!" she cried out. "I saw Vance Martin's brother shoot a rock at Linda with his slingshot. There he goes now!"

Linda and the judges saw the cocky youngster dart away from the arena and disappear. Several other bystanders came up to corroborate the little girl's story.

Linda remained silent, stricken with dismay. Vance's face was red with anger and embarrassment.

One of the judges said kindly, "Please wait a few minutes, Miss Craig."

He conferred in low tones with his associate and the two committeemen. Finally the first judge rose and went over to the loudspeaker.

"Ladies and gentlemen, I have a special announcement to make," he said slowly. "It has been determined that unfair tactics were used against Linda Craig to prevent her winning this event. Since she had passed the last pole with all the rings on her wand, and she made the best time, the judges and committee unanimously declare that Miss Craig is the winner of the Mexican Ring Spearing."

Amid thunderous applause, tears of joy came to Linda's eyes. "Thank you," she said softly.

Then she looked over at the little girl, who was smiling in admiration. Linda beckoned to the child, who ran over. "Thank you, honey, for helping me. I'm very grateful."

Linda was then presented with her trophy. On each corner of its mahogany base stood a small golden horse. In the center was a half dome of gold from which rose a winged mahogany staff bearing the engraved plate. On top of this stood a large parade-type golden horse.

"Hold it!" said a photographer, snapping the scene. Linda smiled, excited and happy.

Many onlookers, including Kathy and the two boys, pressed forward to congratulate Linda and praise Chica d'Oro's performance. Finally, tired but elated, Linda and the others set off for home.

A week later Kathy came over to Rancho del Sol with a package for Linda. "Here's your order," she said, winking.

Bob grinned. "What are you two up to?" he asked. "No more dangerous projects, I hope."

Linda chuckled. "Not yet, Brother. But you and Larry will find out at dinner tonight. How about your inviting him to join us?"

"Will do."

The evening meal proved to be a festive one. After dessert Linda excused herself and left the room. She returned carrying four small, gaily wrapped packages. Smiling, Linda handed one each to Bob, Larry, and Kathy and kept the last for herself.

"Presents?" Larry asked in surprise. "This I like."

"Me too," said Bob. "Do we open them?"

"Of course." Linda laughed.

Doña and Bronco Mallory looked on with interest as the Craigs and their friends unwrapped the boxes. The boys' contained handsome turquoise cuff links.

"Say, these are neat!" Bob exclaimed, holding his up to the light.

"Beauties!" Larry added, highly pleased.

"And I love our rings, Linda," Kathy said, displaying a turquoise stone set in a circle of satiny sterling silver.

"So do I." Linda's eyes sparkled as she slipped hers on.

Bob gave his sister a discerning look. "Don't tell me these were made from bits of turquoise you secretly chipped out in the canyon!"

Linda laughed. "None of you saw me slip a chunk into my boot just before we were captured. I asked Kathy to have her father make these as mementos of our exciting adventure."

Larry grinned and proposed a toast. "Here's to the best detective–rock hound in San Quinto Valley —Linda Craig!"